Cordial Killing

Morewellson, Ltd.

Cordial Killing

A
BACKYARD FARMING
MYSTERY

BOOK 2

VIKKI WALTON

MOREWELLSON, LTD

Morewellson, Ltd.
P.O. Box 49726
Colorado Springs, CO 80949

ISBN: 978-0-9994402-8-5 (standard edition print)

      978-0-9994402-5-4 (e-pub)

Front Cover Illustration: Erika Parker Rogers
Publishing and Design Services:
MartinPublishingServices.com
Formatting: by Rik - Wild Seas Formatting
WildSeasFormatting.com

Cast of Characters

Anne Freemont: Settled into her home in Carolan Springs, Anne's ready for a new challenge with the Brandywine Inn opening next door.

Kandi Freemont (previously Jenkins): Her bubbly personality and killer cooking skills are perfect for the town's new bed and breakfast.

Hope Boswell: Since her father's tragic death, she chose to open the old homestead to guests who visit the tiny mountain town.

Sheriff Carson: Not a fan of newcomer Anne's meddling, he acknowledges her help in solving a case when she first arrived, and he likes her spunk.

Dr. Edward Nelson: His heart condition hasn't stopped his wandering eye or his ways with the ladies.

Elizabeth (Beth) Nelson: Aware of her husband's philandering, she'd do anything to escape the marriage.

Elizabeth (Liz) Latham: Best friends with Beth since college, she harbors a secret that would destroy their friendship.

Elizabeth (Lil) Ryan: Her choice years ago sets off events that could destroy them all.

Christie Taylor: One poor decision made in college would foster a loathing for Edward and change her life forever.

Marie Lawson: Her penchant for gossip and snooping may have caught up to her.

Spencer Andrews: A thirteen-year-old foster boy who always seems to find trouble.

Patricia (Pat) Olsen: Owner of Patty's Pampered Pets.

Stewart Rogers: Inn's handyman, always showing up, especially when Kandi's around.

Sam Powers: EMT and deputy coroner, he hopes to become more than Anne's friend.

Autumn Boettcher: Hope's intern who is gaining hands-on experience in herbalism.

Sorcha Smith: Town's bookstore owner who has sights on Sheriff Carson.

"Every murderer was once someone's old friend."
Agatha Christie

Prologue

Doctor Edward Nelson made his way out to the gazebo, glancing over his shoulder to confirm he hadn't been noticed from the house. He needed time away to think. To decide. To Plan.

He ran his fingers through his hair and across his stubbled jaw. Nearing the gazebo, he glanced back toward the house. He was thankful no one had followed him outside. He couldn't take listening to his faults any longer.

What had she been thinking?

His heart beat faster, but in the last few months he'd become accustomed to the constant irregular rhythm. New medicine had only seemed to aggravate his condition. Or was it something else instead of the medication? He'd felt ill more frequently.

Even his heart seemed to be telling him to get out before it was too late. He knew his cardiac condition would most likely kill him at some point, but what could he do about it? Nothing really. Just keep taking the meds.

He reached into his jacket and felt the glass and metal tube tucked inside. He knew he shouldn't smoke, he was a doctor after all, but he would be damned if he was going to give up every single pleasure he had in life. He wouldn't let her take this, too. He pulled the vape pen from the inner pocket. Quickly glancing back at the house, he felt confident that his vaping would be undetected as long as he kept his back turned. He settled into the chair and crossed his legs. His brow furrowed.

Seeing all four of them together again after all these years brought up memories he had wanted to stay buried. He switched on the electronic cigarette and put it to his mouth. He took a long drag and coughed. More bitter-tasting than usual. His heart picked up the pace.

Edward bent forward, resting his elbows on his knees. He took slow breaths as he waited for his heart to stop racing. Maybe he needed to reduce the percentage of nicotine in the juice. Maybe the propylene glycol and glycerin needed to be higher. Plus, he needed to see what flavoring they'd added. He didn't recall it tasting this bitter before.

I can't take it anymore. I have to get away from her.

Of course, he held a lot of the blame. He knew that. But water under the bridge and all that. No reason to bring it all up again; pick at the scars until they bled.

That's what she wants. She wants to watch me bleed. To suffer.

Anger fueled him.

He rubbed at his eyes and squinted toward the woods at the edge of the property. That had been the impetus for considering retirement. First the heart problems increasing and then having issues with his eyesight. It was time. He wasn't getting any younger. This was the time he could get a good payout from his practice, and with Jake leaving for school, there was no reason to stay working or remain trapped in a dead-end relationship.

He knew she wouldn't go easy. He'd have to make a clean break. Everything and everyone.

A face came to mind. He smiled. Warm memories flew to his mind.

Maybe not everyone.

He sighed. No. Too little, too late.

Edward took another hit from the e-cig. He coughed. His heart raced. He rubbed his chest.

So much wasted time. Wasted life.

He pulled a face. The taste was truly strong and bitter now. The nicotine hit was something he craved, and he would fight through the taste. He wondered if his health was impacting his taste. Things tasted so bitter lately. Once he was back home, he'd get some new vials made up for his vape pen. Possibly something without a flavor.

He took another long drag from the pen and felt the nicotine—no, something else, stronger now—hit his bloodstream. His heart pounded wildly. His hands shook fiercely. He had to get help.

As blackness overtook him, his last thought was *Elizabeth*.

Chapter One

Kandi jumped up and down. "I'm so excited!"

"Really? I couldn't tell." Anne laughed at the young woman's antics. She often wished she had some of Kandi's joyful view on the world. She looked around at the myriad of bags and boxes cluttering the kitchen counters. "Anything I can help with?"

"Nope! I got it all, *like*, under control, Mom." Kandi winked. She grabbed up a bag and pulled open the refrigerator door.

Inside, Anne could see containers marked with the various items and dates. Anne set cartons of creamer and juices on the lone empty shelf. She watched the young woman who hummed as she worked.

Mom. It was the one word Anne never thought she'd hear. Yet in the months since they had taken on the roles of mother and daughter, it still hadn't grown old. "Okay, goof, you'll be sorry when you have lots of boxes to haul over."

"Nope, Stewart said—"

"Oh, Stewart, huh?" Anne lifted her eyebrow and pursed her lips.

"Now don't go starting on that again. He's just a

friend." Kandi folded the bag and set it with a bunch of others inside a box on the floor. She hoisted a box of fire starter logs on her hip and strode toward the front living room. Anne followed behind.

"A charming friend who looks at you with big puppy eyes." Anne made a face and put her hands up mimicking a puppy.

"Nah." Kandi deftly opened the box without breaking a manicured bright fuchsia nail.

"Um, yeah."

"*Like* for real?"

"Yes, like for real. Mark my words, he'll be asking you out soon." She helped Kandi place the starters next to the metal holder filled with cut oak. They were just finishing when they heard a sound in the main hallway.

Hope stood at the front door and called out, "Hey, you two! Are you going to keep chattering or do we have a business to run?"

In unison, Anne and Kandi yelled out, "A business!"

The two-story Victorian had once been home to Hope's father. Set between Kandi's and Anne's houses, the idea to start a partnership and use the old house as a bed and breakfast had quickly gained traction. Ralph had loved growing and eating Brandywine tomatoes so there had been no question of having to think up a name for the new enterprise. Today they would formally open the Brandywine Inn.

Even though it was early May in the mountains, the trio been pleasantly surprised to have their opening weekend almost entirely booked. Two couples and three women had signed up, but one pair canceled at the last minute. Of the five remaining guests, only four would be taking their opening class, "Tinctures, Tisanes, and Tonics."

Hope would be leading this class with Kandi managing all the cooking for the weekend. Anne would assist in helping the guests and taking up the slack where it was needed. She would be in charge of keeping the rooms tidy while the guests were in residence. The women had all admitted that it was exciting and daunting at the same time.

Kandi and Anne reached the large hallway that ran the length of the home with rooms off in either direction. The trio were going over their checklist when a cheery voice caused them to turn around.

"Hello, hello." Marie appeared at the door in the dining room. Anne wondered how long Marie had waited before announcing herself. Hope had let Anne know that Marie loved to listen in on conversations in the hopes of gaining some juicy gossip.

"Hey, Marie," They chimed in unison.

Marie picked up a box she had set next to the large door they had installed in the dining room. The door had been constructed to fit in with the Victorian charm of the old house and it featured beveled glass with *B* and *I* etched into the middle frame. It made a wonderful second entrance if people didn't come in through the main doorway.

In the box Marie held, there were some dried sprigs of elderberry flowers as well as ones with berries that stuck out the edge of the box.

Marie gestured to the box. "I figured I'd bring these over here now, so I wouldn't have to tote them over tomorrow. Where'd you like me to put this?"

"I'll take that." Hope came over and took the box from Marie. "I'm so happy that you have the dried elderberry branches, Marie. They're going to make a wonderful centerpiece for the weekend." She carried the box toward the kitchen as the others followed.

"Would you like a cup of coffee or some tea, Marie?" Kandi opened the cabinet that held colorful mugs with their logo on them.

"That sounds nice. Thank you. Do you have decaf?"

Kandi responded, "Sure. I can make some in a jiff. We got this new cool gadget for making individual drinks. I'd be happy to make you a latte or anything you'd like."

Anne knew that Kandi's easygoing manner would be great with the guests. Anne would have probably said that decaf wasn't worth drinking. Instead she said nothing and simply smiled.

"I'd like a latte with almond milk if it's not too much trouble, Kandi." Hope shifted the box and found a better grip. "Let me just go set this down in the back." She turned toward the back room that was converted into their office and storage room.

"Oh wait." Marie came over and extracted a large decanter from the box. The deep purple liquid barely rippled as she set the bottle down on the table. "The finished product."

"Marie, your elderberry cordial is so awesome it literally blows my mind. I bet that's why it takes the prize at the homesteading fair every year," Kandi exclaimed.

Marie beamed at the praise while Anne bit her tongue at Kandi's use of 'literally.' First, all the *likes*, and now the incorrect use of literally. While the old Anne would have had a sarcastic quip ready on her tongue, she merely thought—*let it go, let it go*.

Hope gingerly took the decanter bottle from Marie and placed it in a place of prominence on a shelf between cabinets. On a shelf below it were some brown-colored bottles filled with who-knows-what concoctions and herbal remedies. She knew that Hope would have them labeled, but had turned the bottles, so that the various colors faced the room.

Anne thought back to her first meeting with Hope when she'd arrived in Carolan Springs. Hope had quickly spotted Anne's health issue. Who knew that hormonal changes could affect her moods . . . and her mouthiness so much?

Anne religiously partook of a tincture and tea mixture that Hope had prepared especially for her. Change of Life: Happy Night Tea had meant no more restless nights or waking up with night sweats. Anne had been hesitant at first, but Hope had managed to convince her that an herbal protocol would be a huge help. Now, Anne was thankful for Hope's expertise and her insight. She felt so much better and had a lot more energy. With that energy came the need to keep her imaginative mind busy. She was still working on remodeling her own home, but she realized she needed something more. She thought of getting a job, but quickly realized the effort and demands it would make on her time. Freedom once tasted, was difficult to give up.

After Ralph's will had been probated, a lot of discussions had gone on at Kandi's kitchen table about the future of the property. Kandi and Anne both hated that they'd be forced to stop using their shortcut to each other's houses when a new owner moved in. Hope had no desire to move there, as she preferred her apartments at the Herbal Shoppe.

Anne couldn't remember who had first come up with the idea of opening a bed and breakfast, but once the seed had been planted, it quickly germinated. Hope, Kandi, and Anne had discussed offering classes on urban homesteading. Anne preferred the term backyard farming or suburban homesteading since Carolan Springs, a town of just over three thousand residents, was undoubtedly not an urban space. In comparison to Denver to the east, the town didn't even rate neighborhood status.

However, during the annual homesteading fair, the town's population and capacity swelled. Opening a bed and breakfast during that time would be a no-brainer. As they talked, they realized they could make more money by hosting backyard farming workshops through the nicer months.

The ladies had decided that each of them would host a workshop about different topics such as raising chickens, bees, and permaculture, as well as indoor skills like making herbal preparations, canning, etc. The guests would learn and see these lessons firsthand at the bed and breakfast. For other areas, like raising goats, they would take day trips to surrounding farms. Because March and April were often designated as "sprinter" by the locals, they decided to launch the program with an indoor class as their inaugural workshop. If winter chose to put on a spring snowstorm, they would still be okay as the classes would all be indoors.

Anne was giddy with excitement about their opening weekend as she had wanted to learn more from Hope about tinctures. She couldn't wait to take part in the workshop and had already staked out an area on her property for some elderberry bushes, which were known to provide great medicinal benefits.

"Anne? Anne." Marie interrupted her thoughts.

"Oh, sorry. Daydreaming. Yes?" Anne turned to where Marie stood next to Kandi.

"Did you hear the news?" Marie's exuberant hand gestures meant she wanted to spill some juicy gossip.

VIKKI WALTON

"What? Did we achieve world peace?" Anne replied, not wanting to fuel Marie's fire, but her snark snuck out anyway. *Shoot.*

Kandi rolled her eyes at Anne behind Marie's back.

"Sorcha and Sheriff Carson broke up. Can you believe it?" Marie grinned in anticipation, waiting eagerly for Anne's response.

"I'm not sure why I should care about that," Anne replied casually, but felt her face becoming flushed.

Geez. Stop it. Nothing like your face and body not cooperating with your 'stay cool' demeanor. Why should I care anyway?

Kandi interjected before Marie could respond, "Here, Marie. Your drink is ready."

Marie nodded and took the cup from Kandi. She sat down at the table.

"You know those types of women are all the same. Love 'em and leave 'em. I mean, really, some of the clothes she wears. If my Grady weren't gone, rest his soul, I'd be locking him up and—"

"And she speaks so highly of you, Marie." Hope cut into Marie's diatribe. Hope leaned against the counter as Kandi focused on pouring almond milk into the steamer cup.

Marie's mouth dropped open as she sought to find a reply. "Well, she's always been nice to me. In fact, I may head on over to the bookstore right now and see what new books have come in lately. Got to support our local businesses, right?"

"Exactly. We're all one big family in this town." Hope gestured with a wave toward the back door. "We'll see you tomorrow. Say around eight, eight-thirty?"

"Yes, looking forward to it." She set her cup in the sink.

After Marie left, the three women stood in silence waiting to hear Marie's car startup. Once they heard the engine, they all broke down laughing.

Anne mimicked, "'And she speaks so highly of you.' Wherever did you come up with that snarky wit, Hope? It's so unlike you."

Hope pointed at Anne. "I learned from the best."

Chapter Two

The morning had flown by. The guests were scheduled to arrive any time after three so Anne decided she would check the guest rooms one more time. She walked up the newly refinished wood stairs that led to the upstairs bedrooms. After they had started remodeling the old home, they found beautiful wood floors under the old carpet throughout. With Stewart's help, they had turned the house into a showcase.

She checked the largest room first. There were two master suites. The largest suite faced the front of the house. Another smaller master suite looked out over the backyard with a beautiful view of the tree line and a sliver of the town's lake shimmering in the distance.

Adjacent to this smaller suite were two rooms with an adjoining shared bath. Across the hall at the far end from the master suite was the largest of the separate rooms with a full bathroom. A much smaller room connected to that room. At one time, this may have been the nursery, and the room next door that of the governess or nursery maid. A powder room and storage closet were also on this floor. At the very end of the hallway was a door that led to a narrow tread staircase that went down to the kitchen and up to the attic. They hadn't bothered doing much work in that area and a sign notified guests of NO ADMITTANCE. Once the weather grew warmer, they planned to paint the steps and the walls a shiny white to help give the area a brighter, cleaner appearance.

Anne stepped to the window. If she looked out toward the right, she could catch a glimpse of snow-covered mountain peaks. Craning her neck out a bit further, Anne could make out the upper story of her own home. With the focus on the new bed and breakfast, she had only remodeled the downstairs and some areas of the top floor. With spring approaching, she hoped to get much more accomplished. If the homesteading fair had as many people attend as last year, she wanted to have rooms ready for any overflow from the bed and breakfast. But, at least she had moved out of the cramped bedroom next to the kitchen.

Anne went through and checked off the list in her head. A goodie basket filled with various locally-produced items as a welcome gift. A note of greeting accompanied the schedule for the weekend. A glass carafe filled with cold water and lemon slices sat on a small table. Beads of sweat had accumulated, and Anne wiped the carafe down with a cloth she had brought up with her. Next to the table, a cabinet held a hot pot with a box of gourmet cocoa and assorted teas. A French press pot with a jar of coffee stood at the ready. A small glass jar contained four of Kandi's awesome melt in your mouth butter cookies. Anne reached down and checked the fridge which held some juice and sparkling water along with a jug of fresh cream.

Taking one last glance at the room, she heard a noise that sounded like footfalls moving down the hallway. She moved away from the cabinet and walked to the door. Anne called out, "Hello?" Neither Kandi nor Hope answered. She looked down the hall. Empty.

One thing about these old houses—they sure make strange noises.

I could have sworn I heard footsteps.

Anne ambled into the next bedroom and began her inspection. After her review of the bathroom, she heard what sounded like someone running down the hall and a door closing. Anne hurried out to the hallway, but again, it was empty.

The hair on her arms stood up. Okay, this is starting to creep me out a bit.

She strode to the banister and leaned over it, but no one was on the stairs. Anne called out again, but no answer returned from downstairs. Then she heard a big thud coming from the back stairs that the servants used. She jogged over to the door of the stairway and swung it open. The smaller landing was empty, as were the stairs.

She could swear she had heard someone running and a thud. She stepped back into the hallway and said aloud, "Look, Ralph, if you've decided to come back as a ghost, now's not a good time, okay?"

"Who you talking to?"

Anne screamed.

Kandi burst out laughing. "What's the matter? Did I, *like*, scare you?"

"No, you didn't *like* scare me. You really scared me! I thought I heard someone running and—was that you?"

She focused her gaze on Kandi. "Have you been hiding out up here?"

"Why would I do that?" Kandi emerald green eyes widened, and she glanced around the hall. "What did you hear? Ooohhhh, do you think it's Ralph's ghost coming back to, *like,* haunt us? Were you literally trying to commune with the dead?"

"No. I don't commune with the dead. Literally or figuratively. You just snuck up on me and scared me. That's all. But we do need to check everywhere to see if there's a loose shutter or something else that's making that noise. We don't want to scare off our first guests before we're even up and running."

"Okay. I'll get Stewart to take a look around."

"Stewart, huh?"

Kandi lifted her hands into a mock action of choking Anne when they heard a car enter the driveway.

They grabbed each other's hands. "They're here!" The pair squealed and rushed down the stairs.

Hope met them at the bottom of the stairs. "Anne, you were right about adding that portico to the side of the house. Looks like they're stopping there."

The neighbors had been okay when Hope and Anne had proposed the bed and breakfast, but multiple cars on the street wouldn't work for the cul-de-sac. While there was plenty of space for parking at the back, they didn't want to welcome guests through the kitchen either. They flipped the dining and living rooms and installed a beautiful doorway in the covered area. This would also work well for finicky Colorado weather. The living room and the dining room both had working fireplaces, so they would be able to keep the ambience they wanted for the Inn.

The trio headed to the door where a sleek silver

Mercedes sat idling in the driveway. Anne recognized the car, as it had been a desired dream car of her first husband; a two-hundred-thousand-plus dream. Anne spied a distinguished looking gentleman with salt-and-pepper hair behind the wheel. This must be Dr. and Mrs. Nelson.

A woman with brunette hair and blonde highlights emerged from the back passenger's side door. Anne guessed the woman was probably Ms. Latham.

"Hello!" She waved. "Where should we park?"

Hope went down the short flight of stairs and stood by the car. The man looked at her but kept his window up. Hope answered and gestured toward the back, "You can park the car there, but for now, this is the place to unload your bags. We can help you take your bags up to your rooms." She motioned toward Anne who stood at the steps. Kandi had gone off to plate up the welcome snacks and get drinks prepared.

The man squinted toward the spot Hope had indicated. He lowered his window. It didn't look like he intended to leave the vehicle. *Was he only dropping them off?* Anne wondered.

Anne skipped down the steps and moved to where Hope and the woman now stood at the back of the car. The trunk opened. The man said something to the other woman in the front passenger seat which sounded like "Get out here and I'll go park the car."

The other woman exited the car, and Anne noticed her surreptitiously wiping her eyes. Was she crying? Oh no, the last thing they needed were marital issues on the first weekend. She glanced over at Hope, who nodded as she had seen it too.

Hope and Anne each grabbed a bag. Mrs. Nelson appeared at the back. Where Ms. Latham's hair was bottle-blonde, Mrs. Nelson was a dark golden blond with some strands of gray peeking through. As she pushed her sunglasses up on her head, her red eyes and blotchy face signaled that Anne had been correct. The woman must have realized how she looked because she opened with, "Hello, sorry about my appearance. I'm fighting some nasty allergies right now. Spring, right?" She smiled, but it didn't reach her eyes.

"Allergies?" Kandi had appeared at the door, and Anne had to quickly intervene before there was a foot-in-mouth episode and they hadn't even made it inside the house yet.

"Yes, those early spring allergies can be killer here in the mountains," Anne replied.

Just then the man rolled his window down and spoke loudly, "Where's the garage?"

Oh geez. Anne and Hope stole glances at each other, their minds on the same thing. Next project—guest garage.

"I apologize." Hope went to his window and gestured toward the back area. "Since these are Victorian homes, they didn't have garages. We don't have one available. However, after the other guests arrive, you can certainly park your car under this portico if you'd like."

He replied in a brusque tone, "I definitely would like. This is two hundred-thousand-dollar vehicle, and I don't want it destroyed by a hailstorm or birds using it for a bathroom."

Great. He's a ray of sunshine. Anne bristled, but luckily Hope replied.

"I can certainly understand your concern. Colorado is known for its crazy weather patterns and its devastating hailstorms. A garage for guests is next on our list of things to incorporate, so thank you for making us aware of it."

Anne had to give it to Hope. She could take any disagreement or surly attitude and smooth things over with her calm manner. No wonder she made a great doctor and herbalist. People knew she wouldn't simply treat them; but would listen and respect them. When Hope's business kept growing, the other doctors in town got concerned. They realized that big city practices of making patients wait for an hour or more, only to be seen for less than fifteen minutes, wouldn't cut it in Carolan Springs. If they wanted their practices to not just survive but thrive, they had to return to practicing a more patient-friendly style of medicine. Younger doctors who preferred a hybrid and preventative approach were flocking to the area and starting up small practices which left them with a better life and work balance too.

Anne moved over and set a piece of heavy luggage on the steps to the house. Hope stood next to Dr. Nelson's window, speaking in slow, soothing tones.

"Again, just for now, if you'll kindly pull the car to the back until the others arrive. If you leave us the keys, we would be happy to move it for you."

He grumbled under his breath about no one driving his car. Hope stepped back as he put the car in drive, the trunk still open.

Hope avoided looking at Anne and instead took in a deep cleansing breath, which Anne knew was Hope's way of calming herself. Hope beamed at the two women who each held smaller bags. "Please ladies, follow me." Hope grabbed two bags and headed into the doorway with the two women following. Anne waited and took up the rear. As the women mounted the steps, she saw Ms. Latham patting Mrs. Nelson's arm and whispering, "It will all work out. Don't worry."

What will work out? Anne groaned inwardly at the prospect of walking on eggshells all weekend around the Nelsons.

Hope took Mrs. Nelson to the master suite facing the front of the house since it was the largest of all the rooms.

"Follow me." Anne gripped the bag tighter in her hand and moved down the hall to the last room on the left. The woman followed her, glancing at the doors Anne pointed out along the way.

"This first door is to a smaller bedroom for when we have guests with children. It will be empty while you're here." Anne pointed to the next door. "That's a small powder room." She inclined her head toward the doors on the other end of the hall which led to additional guest rooms. They reached the end of the hall. The servant's door had the NO ADMITTANCE plaque on it.

"Where does that go?" Miss Latham inquired.

"It's the stairway that goes down to the kitchen and back office. We ask that guests not use these stairs as they are narrow, and the passage is dark. However, we don't lock it because of fire safety. Should you need to exit this floor and the front staircase is blocked, you could use this one."

"Good to know. You never know when you might need to escape." She cocked her eyes back toward where the Nelsons would be staying and laughed. Anne forced herself to hide her smirk by opening the door to the room. After acquainting the woman with the room, she departed and met Hope on the stairs. They said nothing as they made their way downstairs to await the next round of guests. Kandi came in from the kitchen and joined Hope and Anne in the back office.

Anne spoke first. "What a jerk."

"Don't hold back now. Tell me what you really think." Hope laughed.

"I hope he isn't going to be like this all weekend. He didn't even get out of his car to unload the bags or help his wife."

"He may have been having withdrawals. I was looking out the kitchen window when he, *like,* pulled his car up to the back. He got out and went over between the gazebo and the lilac bushes. I saw that new kind of cigarette-thingy, so I think he wanted a smoke," said Kandi. She wiped her hands on the towel she held and spoke to herself. "I hope it has, *like,* some 'quit-being-a-jerk' juice in it."

"Hmmm, I think we can figure out that you think he's a jerk," Anne quipped. "Maybe he has a bad back or is all for women empowerment."

"Whatever." Kandi sat down on the bench by the window and tucked her feet up under herself. "You ever get a feeling that you just don't like someone? That's what I get with him." She wrapped her arms around a pillow. "I hope he doesn't, *like,* ruin our first weekend."

"Well, at least she has her friend with her." Anne pulled up the registration forms. "I wonder why he came at all if he didn't want to be here."

"Not a clue, but I'm sure we're going to find out. Unfortunately." Hope ran her hands through her pixie cut.

The sound of another car's engine let them know the second group of guests had arrived. Both women stood together and crossed their fingers.

Outside, under the portico, a buxom lady with short curly hair of an indeterminate reddish color was extracting herself from the vehicle. She stretched her back with both hands situated firmly on her broad hips. She yawned loudly.

As she glimpsed the women stepping out of the Inn, the woman straightened her posture.

"Howdy." She strode over to them and grasped Anne's hand in a hearty handshake. "I'm Taylor. Where should I park the old girl?" The 'old girl' was an older model Jeep that looked like it had been around the block far more than a few times.

"You can park out in the back next to the Mercedes, but you can unload your bags here."

"Did ya hear that, Lil? You can get out here." Taylor walked to the back of the car and unlatched the back door. It swung up revealing an old duffle bag next to a smart new roller bag.

The passenger appeared at the edge of the vehicle. As different as night and day to the first woman, this woman was petite and slim with an ethereal beauty that shone out from some hidden source. Her blue eyes were set in a doll-like face with porcelain skin, and her white-gold hair shone like an angel. The woman wore no makeup or, if she did, it was minimal. Other than her friend, Eliza, Anne had rarely seen such a naturally beautiful woman.

As Anne and Hope gathered up their bags, a crash sounded behind them. Mrs. Nelson stood in the vestibule to the open door outside. Her gaze was fixed on Lil. At her feet, a broken glass dripped water on the floor.

A sharp intake of breath also came from Lil.

Anne and Hope locked eyes. This didn't bode well for the opening of the Brandywine Inn.

Chapter Three

Kandi emerged from the kitchen, saw the mess on the floor, and retreated back to the kitchen. She quickly returned with a broom and dustpan. Mrs. Nelson made a short apology and quickly vanished back to her room upstairs.

As Kandi cleaned up the glass, Hope and Anne escorted Lil and Taylor to their rooms. Anne hoped that Mrs. Nelson would be in her room, as it appeared that some issues needed addressing before the official start of the weekend.

Anne had returned downstairs. "What in the—! This group just keeps giving and giving—and not in a nice way!" she said to Hope and Kandi back in the office. She leaned on the door jamb. "What are we missing here? Something is definitely rotten in Denmark."

"What's Denmark, *like*, got to do with it?" Kandi asked innocently.

"You know, Hamlet, ghost," Anne replied.

"What? You think she saw a ghost and it made her drop the glass?" Kandi's lip quivered.

"No. Never mind, sweetie." Anne faced Hope. "What's your take on it, Hope?"

"Looks like someone was extremely surprised to see the other someone. Both Mrs. Nelson and Lil had very strong reactions at seeing each other."

"What do you think is the best course of action?" Anne opened a drawer and dug around to find the house checkbook. She held it up. "Refund?"

"I don't think we're there yet, but we do need to find out what's going on before the group meets up. Let's have a chat with Taylor. She didn't seem bothered and I think she may know something about what's going on."

Anne and Kandi nodded in agreement.

Hope rang Taylor's room and asked if she would be available to come down to the library off the dining room for a welcome chat. "I'll be back in a jiff. Just need to pop home for a minute." Anne went to her house to check on Mouser and set up the kitty's dinner treat in the timer tray. Turning on some lights for the evening, she went back to the Inn where she found Taylor and Hope sitting in seats across from one another. Hope was listening to something when Anne walked in.

"Oh, hey, Anne," Taylor spoke up. "I was just telling Hope here that I guess it looks like me and Liz have some explaining to do." She stretched out her legs and crossed her feet at the ankles. Her scuffed cowboy boots were long broken in. She leaned forward and grasped her calf.

"Let's see. Where to start? You see we were all close friends in college. As you can probably tell, I'm from Texas, or maybe ya'll can't." She winked. "Anyway, all the rest of the gals were from up north. We were best buds—them all sharing the same name and me using my last name."

The confusion on Anne's and Hope's face must have registered because Taylor went on speaking.

"You know, 'Elizabeth.' They all share the same name. In our first class, a professor asked Elizabeth to answer, and all three chimed in. To say it was more confusing than a rafter's body floating on the Frio is an understatement."

She laughed heartily at the confusion on their faces. "Ahhh. You probably never been rafting." They both shook their heads to the negative.

"Well, let's just say that your hiney is sitting in what amounts to icebox cold water and your top is in a hot, humid oven that's cooking you." She slapped her hand on her leg. "Loads of fun."

"Um, thanks for that. Now back to the school and names," Anne coaxed.

"Sure 'nuff. As ya'll know, I'm Christie Taylor. When we were in school, we were often kidded about it, and they'd call our group Elizabeth Taylor. Nowadays, half the kids never even heard of Elizabeth Taylor. Anyhoo, I was the only one that didn't have to come up with a nickname as teachers often use your last name anyway. But they all chose a name to be called by in class. Beth already had hers from home, so you have Beth, Lil, and Liz." Taylor uncrossed her ankles as a knock sounded on the door.

It was Liz. After settling into a chair, she spoke to Taylor. "I think we may have put our foot in it. I never, ever thought Lil would come." She turned to Anne and Hope. "I'm not sure what Taylor's told you, but there'd been a falling out back in college. I figured that it was time to make amends and let bygones be bygones. I mean, we're talking over twenty years. I really missed Taylor and asked her to come for a visit."

"Of course," Taylor took up the dialogue, "We couldn't have a proper reunion without Lil. I meant to break it to her a bit better than it went down." She faced Liz, and her tone grew angry. "And what's with having *him* come? You never said he was coming."

"I'm sorry about that. I talked to Beth about getting away for a weekend—a girls' getaway—and she said she wanted Eddie—I mean, Edward, to come too." She lowered her voice, "To keep him out of trouble." Then she laughed, "You know, men. She didn't want to leave him home, in case he'd gotten a new . . . toy." She shrugged.

New toy? What was Liz implying?

"Well, ain't this a fine kettle of fish we got here. What should we do?" Taylor popped up from her chair and paced the room.

Anne and Hope realized they'd been relegated to simple bystanders. They exchanged looks. If one or more guests left and wanted refunds, they wouldn't break even for the weekend on all the food and other items they had purchased for the class. Some things could be reused, but others would just be a loss. Anne sighed. Ideas, plans, and reality seldom intertwine.

Liz responded, "How about this? I'll go talk to Lil and then speak to Beth. Maybe we can help them see this is a good idea. What do you think, Tay? I want to make sure you stay involved with what happens."

"Suits me. But shouldn't I be the one to talk to Lil?" She crossed her arms.

"No. I think it will be better if I do the talking. If you trust me, then I'm sure I have a solution that will work." Liz stood. "Don't worry ladies. I've got this under control and I'm determined that this weekend is going to solve everything."

"But what about *him*?" Taylor's distaste for Dr. Nelson evident in her tone.

"Don't worry. I can handle him. He only came because this gives him an *out* for going on an upcoming golf trip to Atlanta. He won't be attending the workshops so the only times he'll be around will be at breakfast, if at that. Plus, it's only a few days and I know this will be resolved. That won't be too bad, will it?"

Only a few days. Anne would have to hold on to those words for what looked to be some difficult days ahead.

Chapter Four

Four-thirty.

That was the time when they would give an overview of the weekend. Kandi had arranged little plates of hors d'oeuvres on the sideboard along with various drinks. She had changed into a cute red-and-white polka-dot dress and let her cherry-red hair spill over her shoulders. She accessorized with two butterfly clips that held her hair back off her freckled face.

"You look so pretty, honey." Anne hugged Kandi.

"Thanks, Mom."

Was there ever a sweeter sound? If so, Anne didn't know what it would be. Last year when she had asked Kandi to allow her to adopt her, it had been an earnest gesture. Even though Kandi was a woman in her twenties, both wanted desperately to belong to a family. So, Kandi changed her last name from Jenkins to Freemont. Anne had set up a trust so that all her belongings and intellectual property rights for her books would go to Kandi. Not that Kandi needed it. She was coming into millions left to her mother who had deserted Kandi and her younger twin brothers as children. It also didn't hurt to have a different last name now that Kandi's ex-husband had become a long-term resident of Cañon City.

Hope came down the hallway carrying a tray of glasses filled with sparkling water and lime slices or mint. Taylor stepped into the room, her commanding presence reminded Anne of a no-nonsense, take-charge individual. Lil's footsteps were quiet as a cat's as she followed Taylor into the room. She had changed from her earlier outfit and now wore a white cashmere sweater over white pants. She wore small silver studs in her tiny ears, now visible due to the simple chignon revealing her milky white neck.

Striking. That's the word that came unbidden to Anne's mind. While Taylor plopped into one of the big overstuffed chairs, Lil gracefully lowered herself into the mahogany Queen Anne chair in the corner, next to the desk facing toward the door.

"Would you care for a drink?" Hope offered to Taylor first and then took the tray over to Lil. Taylor took a few gulps as Lil sipped hers slowly.

"This is mighty refreshing." Taylor held up her glass with mint.

"Yes, it's essential to drink lots of water in Colorado due to the altitude. If you don't stay hydrated, you can get headaches from dehydration and become ill. So that's the first thing we offer."

"It's very nice." Lil's soft voice answered back.

Anne was about to get up and go see where the other three guests were when they heard the side door open. Stewart walked in.

"Oh, sorry. Didn't mean to intrude." He took off his cap and smoothed down his hair, missing one spot that Anne struggled not to reach up and put in place.

"Stewart, all well?" Hope went over and gave him a friendly hug.

"Stewart. Good to see you," Anne interjected.

He nodded back at her. "Good to see you too."

Hope turned and faced the women. "Ladies, this is Stewart. He is our handyman. We've had a shutter banging so we asked him over to get things all nailed down for us."

Taylor rose quickly from her chair and shook his hand. "Hey Stewart, I'm Taylor, and this is my good friend, Lil."

As Stewart's mouth gaped at the woman, Lil remained seated in her chair and merely nodded. Anne figured Lil was used to the affect she had on men. She almost wanted to bean Stewart over the head on behalf of Kandi, with that look he had on his face. Even though Lil was at least twice his age, her beauty seemed to affect all ages.

Sensing a presence behind them, they turned to see that Dr. Nelson, Beth, and Liz had arrived. They stood at the edge of the door. The atmosphere became charged with an undercurrent of so many emotions—anger, passion, even fear—that it felt as real as if another person had entered the room.

Hope and Anne stood still, not knowing what the best way would be to break the spell. Stewart stepped forward and introduced himself to the trio. After those exchanges had finished, Steward excused himself and left.

Taylor spoke next. "Well look at what the cat drug

in. Old Doc himself. I'd have thought some husband would have shot you by now."

Anne stiffened. Yikes. She turned to Hope, whose own face mirrored her own surprise.

"Ah, still the same old—" His gaze had found Lil. He swallowed. Hard.

Beth reached over and put her arm possessively around his. There was no mistaking her gesture. He pushed her off. Evidently, he didn't appreciate the motion.

Lil had dropped her gaze and focused on the mint in her drink.

Liz broke the silence. "Well, the gang's all here. It's like old times—Elizabeth and Taylor."

"Where can I get a drink?" Dr. Nelson turned to Anne. Hope picked up a couple of glasses and walked over to the group.

"Here you are." She handed one to him and one to Beth.

He took a sip. "Don't you have anything stronger?" He hoisted the glass in the air.

"Ed, you know alcohol isn't good for you," Beth replied.

"Mind your own business. I'm not a kid." He snarled at her.

"Your funeral. Sooner would be my preference." Beth muttered under her breath as Liz led her to over to a loveseat and sat down beside her. Dr. Nelson remained standing and Anne noticed him steal a glance over at Lil every once in a while.

"Still the same old sweet guy I see," Taylor retorted, heading to Anne for a refill.

"Taylor, cut the—"

"Ladies! And Sir," Hope inclined her head toward

him. They needed to stop this conversation before it got even worse.

"Thank you for coming to our inaugural opening of the Brandywine Inn. We hope you thoroughly enjoy your stay here and that you learn a few things about making tinctures, tisanes, and tonics at home. Marie will be joining us tomorrow and the day will focus on the elderberry plant and its many medicinal and edible uses. I will be sharing about herbalism in the morning, and then we will go on to make some of the products in the afternoon."

"Not me," Edward Nelson interjected, "I'm a real doctor and don't believe in all this hooey."

"Well," Hope struggled to keep her composure, "I'm a *real* doctor too. I have my MD from Johns Hopkins. However, I also believe that the body can best be served, and optimal health achieved, through preventative medicine. Thus, I chose to continue my education, so I double majored in herbal sciences and nutrition at Bastyr.

"Looks like she told you," Taylor quipped, taking another long drink to hide her chuckling.

Anne went over and touched Hope on the arm. They had decided on using this as a signal where the other one would take over if they found themselves getting frustrated with a guest.

"Okay, ladies, I know that you're in for a treat on the next few days. Tonight, you're free to roam around the town, and we'd be happy to provide you with some ideas for dinner places if you'd like some recommendations. There is also a list in your guest welcome book in your rooms. We don't have a liquor license, and we decided not to get one to answer your question on that, Mr. Nelson."

"Doctor."

"Geez, Edward." Liz shook her head.

"My apologies. Of course, *Doctor* Nelson." Anne nodded her head. She turned back to the others. "We do ask that you drink plenty of water to stay hydrated. There is water up in your rooms and just in case you run out, we have an area down in the dining area where you can get water, coffee, tea, and various things like soft drinks or juices during the day or night.

"We have two options for you in the morning depending on early or later risers. For those who would like to take a walk in the morning, we'll be going on the trail behind the house and walk over to the lake. My friend Eliza, who is out of town, has offered to let us use her deck area. It's a beautiful place to see the lake with the sun hitting the mountains in the distance. Sometimes if you're lucky you can catch sight of a moose in the distance or other animals coming down to the lake to drink."

"What time is that?" Beth interjected.

"If we could start out just before six, we'll get the best view," Hope responded.

"Six in the morning?" Beth replied, "I'll pass."

"Why? It's not like you're getting any beauty sleep," Edward replied.

"Edward! Enough," Liz retorted and put her arm around Beth, giving her a side hug.

Lil spoke in a quiet, yet commanding, tone, "I'd like to go. It sounds lovely."

"Me too! I've always wanted to see a moose out in the wild." Taylor raised her glass.

"Why not? I'm in." Edward glanced over at Beth.

Liz twisted in her seat. "I'll stay with you Beth, if you want to sleep in and hang around here."

"No!" It had come out more forcefully than Beth had probably expected, and Liz scooted back. "I'm going too."

"Okay, that sounds great." Hope smiled at the group. "We'll meet at ten minutes before six in the morning. Please wear comfy walking shoes and layers. Of course, bring your jacket. If you have gloves and a hat, bring those too. The weather this time of year is still cold in the morning, but you'll warm up as you walk. Also, the trail is pretty flat, but there may be some snowy spots in the shady areas, so be prepared for that."

Kandi popped her head in the door and waved. "Hi, you all. I'm going to be preparing your breakfast while you're gone, so come back with a hearty appetite. Tomorrow we're going to have a frittata for the savory side and a stuffed French toast with elderberry syrup for the sweet side. Do you all prefer bacon, sausage, or both?"

"Sounds yummy. I'd like a bit of all of it," replied Taylor.

"Second that," Liz and Beth responded in unison.

Dr. Nelson moved toward Kandi, his voice taking on a sickly-sweet quality, "I'd rather just have some fried eggs. Think you can help me out with that, pretty girl?"

"Certainly, sir." Kandi grimaced and stepped back as he moved to touch her arm.

Anne popped over by Kandi's side. "I think that's everyone. You can go now, sweetie."

"You forgot someone," Beth spoke up. "Lil,"—it was the first time she'd acknowledged the other woman's presence—"what do you want?"

The group all turned toward Lil.

The petite woman didn't respond to Beth's question but addressed Kandi. "Kandi, thank you for everything.

I'm not looking for anything special. I'm perfectly content with whatever you prepare."

Anne looked back and forth between the pair wondering if this part of the conversation had been about breakfast choices or something more. All she knew was that she couldn't wait to talk with Hope and Kandi about it.

Chapter Five

"I was going to save this until after the weekend was over, but I think we might need it now." Hope uncorked a bottle of prosecco and started pouring into champagne flutes.

"Geez, the nerve of that guy." Anne took a sip of the bubbly drink. "I don't know why he and Beth are married."

"He, *like,* creeps me out," Kandi responded. "But I like Taylor. She doesn't take any guff from him, and I literally thought his head was going to explode when she chewed him out in front of everyone."

"You literally thought his head was going to explode?" Anne quipped, shaking her head.

"Huh?" Kandi plopped back on the couch cushions. "Oh wait, are you being facetious again?"

"You know I love you, you goof." Anne plopped down next to Kandi.

"Love you, *like,* too." Kandi giggled and bumped her shoulder against Anne's.

Hope chose the overstuffed chair where Taylor had sat earlier. She shucked off her Bob's flats with the cat pattern on them and tucked her legs up in the chair. "While I would normally gag over your sugary love fest, I have to say it's refreshing after the last few hours. I probably haven't had a better moment today. Except maybe when both cars drove away."

"So, what do you all, *like,* think the real story is about them all? If they all hate each other, why spend the weekend together?" Kandi took off her shoes and tucked her feet up like Hope.

Anne scooted back and stuck her feet up on a nearby ottoman. "I think that someone—either Taylor or Liz—is trying to heal old wounds. What they are is anyone's guess, but my money's on Lil trying to steal Edward from Beth."

"Don't you mean *Doctor?*" Hope made air quotes with her fingers.

"I'm proud of you for not bopping him over the head right then and there. What a pompous jerk. I don't know what happened, but don't you find it weird that they all have the same name?"

"What do you mean?" Kandi cocked her head.

"They all have the same name—Elizabeth. Except of course, for Taylor. At school, they were often referred to as Elizabeth Taylor, you know, like the actress."

"Hmm. Never heard of her. What movie has she been in lately?" Kandi looked at Anne.

"Argh." Anne grabbed a couch pillow and hit Kandi with it. "This is exactly what I mean about you young whippersnappers."

"What's a whippersnapper?"

"Truthfully, I have no idea, but you're one of them."

Kandi looked confused.

Hope got up and held the bottle up questioningly. "More?"

"That's it for me. We're going to need to be on our toes with these folks."

BAM!

Kandi screamed and jumped off the couch. "What was that?"

"Oh no. You don't think they're back and heard us talking about them? That would be awful." Anne grimaced.

Hope jogged to the door by the portico. "Nope. I didn't think so but wanted to check just to be sure. Where do you think it came from?"

"You know, I heard some noise upstairs earlier today." Anne set her glass down next to Hope's. "At first, I thought one of you had come upstairs. But when I looked in the hall, no one was there. Then I went in to check the other room and thought I heard someone running down the hall. When I went back out to check it, again, no one was there."

"Ooooh, I don't like this." Kandi hugged her arms. "Do you think Ralph doesn't like our idea and is haunting us?"

"Don't be silly. I'm sure there's some reasonable explanation, but we do need to figure out what's causing it. Stewart took a quick look and said he couldn't find anything, but he'll be back when he has more time." Hope moved to the door. "Since it sounded like it came from upstairs, let's go take a look."

Anne followed behind with Kandi whimpering, "Wait for me. I don't want to be, *like*, alone."

The trio took the wide wood front stairs to the

second landing and looked through all the rooms. Nothing.

"Do you think we should check the servant back stairs?" Hope asked Anne.

"I don't see how anything could make that sound in there, but it wouldn't hurt." They opened the door to the narrow set of wooden stairs that led down to the kitchen. Again, nothing. A door to the attic stood a bit ajar.

"I bet that's it." Hope pointed to the door. "You know these old houses. Everything is off balance. Maybe the wind caught the door and it slammed shut."

"The wind? In a stairway?" Anne made a face. "Seriously? That's your reasoning?"

Kandi shivered. "I'm getting scared."

"There's nothing to be scared about. There's some reasonable explanation for the noises." She turned back to Hope. "I know we've been storing some stuff up in the attic rooms. Stewart has also been working on the shutters. Do you think some boxes fell over up there?"

Hope nodded her head. "Makes sense. I guess we could go see." The trio looked at the gaping door and the darkness beyond, but no one made an effort to open it further.

"Look, we're all tired, and we have a busy day tomorrow. We can get Stewart to check it out up there tomorrow."

Hope and Kandi both agreed and all three pretended not to be spooked as they closed the door to the set of back stairs that servants employed at the turn of the century.

As they went back down the main stairs, Anne wondered if this bed and breakfast concept had been such a good idea. She knew it was a way to keep the path between her and Kandi's houses clear. It also would allow her to create a bigger food forest guild in her own yard and more traditional gardening spaces in Ralph's old yard. When they had contemplated the idea between them, they all quickly agreed that it could only have one name. Ralph had loved his Brandywine tomatoes. Those very tomatoes were the reason behind Anne and Kandi meeting for the first time. She could never have imagined the many changes that had occurred in her life over these last months. Now she was officially the mother of a daughter and an innkeeper. She sighed with contentment.

"You okay?" Kandi glanced worriedly at Anne.

Anne smiled at her. "Yes, very. I'm happy."

"You know, even though our first guests have been less than nice, I'm happy too." Hope hugged Anne and then Kandi in turn. "To wonderful partners."

"To partners," They chimed.

Hope moved toward the back door. "I've got to go home for a bit and check to see how Autumn's doing with mom."

"Autumn?"

"Yes, oh I forgot. Autumn is here from Bastyr interning for me. This works well as the shop can stay open while I'm teaching the classes. I told her I'd get someone to sit with mom, but she said not to worry. Missy, Sorcha's daughter, is coming over and they're going to be playing Settlers of Catan. The new medication mom's taking helps her stay more alert for a longer time, so she'll enjoy their company."

Anne recalled how Faith had never revealed to Hope that Ralph was her father. He had paid for Hope's medical studies and tried to help Faith when the first signs of her dementia appeared. But the elderly woman refused to accept the assistance. Because she'd been visiting Ralph at his house without Hope's knowledge, this was another reason to keep the home. With Kandi as the cook, Hope owning the house, and Anne with her business acumen, it had all fallen into place. Kandi, with a bit of help from Anne's prestige as an author of homesteading books, had seen the last homesteading fair fill up every available hotel in town. They figured they would keep it open in the busier times and close down over the snowy winter season.

"Hope," Kandi tilted her head, "how are you getting home?"

"I can walk back." She tugged on her navy peacoat.

Anne looked outside into the darkness. "I need to go into town and grab a few things at the store. Let me drive you. Kandi, can you hold down the fort until we get back?"

"And leave me, *like,* all alone here? Um, no thanks."

"Fine. I'll stay here, and you can go run the errands for me then."

Kandi grabbed her jacket from the back hook. "What do you need?"

"A couple of cans of cat food for Mouser. But not the chicken, she prefers the salmon ones."

Kandi laughed. "Yeah, so who didn't want a cat and now it's, *like,* probably the most spoiled animal in our town?"

"She's not the most spoiled. Maybe the second most spoiled." Anne chuckled. Kandi was right. She hadn't wanted any animals, and now Mouser would curl up on her lap nightly while she read or wrote. Mouser had quickly put all the mice in the old Victorian on notice that they weren't welcome. Anne was happy not to have to deal with a mouse invasion once winter had arrived.

"Hey ladies, we should probably get a move on.

Because of our early start tomorrow I'm going to spend the night. I'll use the cubby in our office." Hope pulled on a cloche-style hat in a flattering shade of maroon.

Knowing that they might need to have someone occasionally spend the night, even with Anne and Kandi both living next door, they divided up the old maid's quarters downstairs into the office, a bathroom, and space just large enough for a twin bed.

Anne agreed. With this group, it would be best to have someone on the premises. "Sounds good. Kandi can get my list, and I'll hang out here until you all get back from town."

After Hope and Kandi left, Anne cleaned the glasses and set out the cups and place settings for tomorrow's breakfast. Better to get ahead of things if tomorrow proved as trying as today had been.

She decided to go upstairs and check the rooms. She took a plastic bag for trash and a carryall bucket that held chocolate treats for turndown service.

Entering Lil's room, Anne found it not very different than its original appearance. Lil's clothing had been hung in the closet and toiletries stacked neatly by the sink. Anne turned down the bed, laid a local gourmet chocolate on the pillow, and went through the adjoining bathroom door into Taylor's room. Clothing had been flung on chairs and the bed. Toiletries were all over the bathroom counter, hurriedly pulled from a cosmetic bag. Anne straightened the bed, pulled back the cover, and placed the chocolate on the pillow.

Finally, with a sense of hesitation, she entered the Nelsons' room. Both bags sat on the luggage stands, open but unpacked. She quickly turned down the king-size bed and placed a piece of chocolate on each pillow. She then went to the bathroom to empty the trash. She dumped the bin into the plastic bag and then started for the bedroom. On the floor next to the wastebasket, Anne spied a crumpled-up piece of paper.

She picked it up and hesitated on throwing it in the trash bag. Maybe it was something they needed. She set the bag down and opened the paper.

It read, "It's your turn to suffer now."

Who had written the note and who had been the intended recipient—Edward or Beth?

She stuck it in her pocket and left the room. This really put a twist on things. She needed to speak to Hope when she returned.

Arriving back down in the kitchen, she placed the trash in the bin when headlights illuminated the driveway. Deciding to set a better tone for the rest of the evening, Anne headed to the back door to the porch, just as a woman's scream punctured the air.

Chapter Six

Anne flew down the steps over to where Beth stood with her mouth open, pointing toward the tree line.

"I saw a bear! I saw a bear!"

Liz had exited the back seat and was now standing next to the shaken woman. She spoke something in a comforting voice.

Edward had exited the car and was squinting at the trees. "I don't see anything. You sure you didn't imagine it?"

"NO! I did not imagine it. It was big and brown, and its eyes looked right at me. I hate this place." She jerked free from Liz's arms and railed at her, "Why did you bring us here? First, I have to contend with seeing *that* woman after all these years, and now there are bears. What were you thinking?" The vitriol poured from Beth. Liz took a step back, an undefinable emotion registering on her face.

"I'm so sorry, Beth." She held her hands up as if surrendering. "I thought this would be a nice getaway. I didn't expect Taylor to bring Lil. I knew you were interested in this herbal stuff. Come on. It will be fun."

Anne chimed in, "I know that Hope and Marie have prepared a great workshop for you. As for the bear, this is Colorado, and you can see wildlife. I'm wondering if it wasn't another animal though, since bears normally stay on the southern side of the lake after waking from hibernation."

Edward laughed. "There you go. It was some animal, but not one that will eat you. Now, if you all will excuse me, I'm going to bed." He stalked off, leaving the three women behind.

Beth moved over toward Anne. "I'm sorry. I shouldn't have acted like that, and I'm sorry for the early stuff as well. Just seeing—well, it doesn't matter. It's no excuse for my behavior. I am looking forward to the classes." She turned to Liz. "Will I see you upstairs?"

Liz nodded. "I'll be up in a bit. I think I may see about getting a cup of chamomile tea."

"Okay. Well, goodnight. I'll see you tomorrow." She went over and hugged Liz. Anne heard her say a whispered sorry to the woman.

As soon as they had gone in, Taylor and Lil arrived back at the house. Anne tensed. Was another showdown about to commence?

Taylor spoke first. "Hiya. That was a great restaurant you recommended."

"Yes, it was very nice," Lil agreed. "Thank you." Lil acknowledged Liz with a quick nod and moved on to the door. "Good night everyone."

Taylor faced Liz. "Give me the real enchilada, Liz. What's up with your bright idea to bring these two frenemies together? I thought you'd squared it with Beth and Lil and then I show up to this. I almost expected a knock-down, drag-out fight between Beth and Lil earlier." Taylor crossed her arms over her ample bosom and raised her eyebrows. Anne wouldn't have liked to have Taylor for a teacher. She started thinking about what she could confess even if she were innocent.

"Listen, I told Beth that we've all moved beyond old school crushes and heartaches. That now's the time to make amends. Sure, our paths might not ever cross again, but they could. Plus, I've been missing you and Lil."

"Quit blowing smoke up my dress," Taylor wisecracked.

Quit...what? Anne stared at the imposing woman.

"I'm not. I'm serious." Liz held up her hands. "Look. I just think she's tired."

Taylor uncrossed her arms. "I bet she is. She and old Doc are like fire and gasoline. I don't understand why they ever got married." She stopped. "Well, actually I do. He wanted the sun but settled for the moon."

Anne realized at that moment what had been tickling the edge of her mind. Beth was a pale imitation of Lil, whose beauty shone from her. She stole a glance at the house. Two women. One man. Had Lil been the one to write the letter she'd found in the Nelsons' room? And if she had, who had been the intended recipient?

She realized Liz was speaking to her. "Um, sorry?"

"I was wondering about some chamomile tea?"

"Oh, yes, of course. Taylor, would you like some hot tea before bed?"

"Don't mind if I do."

A man's voice startled them. "What kind do you have?"

Dr. Nelson must have come back outside while they

were chatting. Had he heard their conversation? He had to have gone out through the kitchen door as they would have seen him through the glass door opening to the portico. Kandi had been right earlier. He had probably gone out for a smoke out in the back. But why the secrecy? If Anne was right, Beth didn't like his smoking any more than any of his other habits.

Before Anne could respond, Liz spoke, "You sneaking out to smoke again?"

"What's it to you, Liz?"

"Nothing. But you know Beth asked you to stop. It's not good for my heart."

Hmmm. Was that a Freudian slip? Liz had said my heart versus your heart. Was there now or had there been something between the two?

"You know I've switched to this stupid thing." He pulled the vape pen from his shirt pocket.

Taylor moved over and pulled it from his hand. She shook it in his face. "This thing will kill you. It's no better than regular cigarettes." She held it out in front of him and he retrieved it.

Liz implored, "Just don't let Beth see, okay? How about trying to get along for once in your life. At least for this weekend?"

"I'm going out to the gazebo where she can't see me, so don't get your panties all in a wad over what's none of your business."

"None of my—" Anne watched as Liz clamped her lips together, silencing a retort.

He nodded at the group. "Ladies."

"Let's go get you all some tea. We have an early morning start." Anne gestured to the house. Inside, she started the hot pot and placed the assortment of teas out for selection. Liz was adding some honey to her tea when they heard honking from a car horn outside.

"That's strange. This cul-de-sac is usually very quiet." Anne went and opened the front door and peered out. Kandi's bright red pickup was at the curb and Hope was exiting the vehicle. Kandi waved. "See you tomorrow!" She put the truck in gear and Anne watched as she pulled the truck into her driveway and disappeared to the back.

Hope reached the steps. Anger radiated from her.

"What's up?" Anne took the grocery bag from her.

"Some dumb kid almost got himself killed, that's what. He was wearing all black, and he ran right in front of Kandi's truck. It's a good thing she spotted him."

"Hmmm, who do you think it was and what was he doing over here this late?"

"Well, we did have that issue of kids breaking into the house after Ralph died."

Anne thought back to when that very thing had almost landed her in jail right after she had moved to Carolan Springs.

"He can obviously see the house is lit up and people coming and going. Plus, we have the new sign on the front porch. Maybe he'll tell all his friends, and we won't have to worry about any more vandalism."

"True. But it was weird that he was running toward the house instead of away from it." Hope handed Anne the bag from the store containing cat food and a bottle of kefir.

"Listen, can you come over to my place, so we can chat about today? I think we need to get our ducks in a row before tomorrow."

"I'll say." Hope ran a finger across her throat. "The words 'why did you open an inn' were on auto-repeat in my mind all day."

They shut and locked the front door and walked across the two gravel drives to Anne's house. As they rounded the house and walked up to the back door, Anne smiled to herself. This old house had started everything for her. A new beginning that had led to new friends, a loving daughter, a business enterprise, and a life she had always wanted. If it hadn't have started out with a dead body, knocks to the head, nasty encounters with the local sheriff, and a glimpse into the darkness of the human soul, it would have been pretty perfect.

Anne unlocked her back door. Unlike many in the town that rarely locked their doors, she was from the East Coast, and she preferred the security of a locked door. Inside the house, she took off her shoes and shoved her feet into fuzzy pink slippers. She walked past the old scullery area and into the kitchen where a hungry Mouser welcomed her with a swipe up against her legs and a loud admonition about being late for dinner.

"You'd think you were starving to death, you silly girl." Anne picked up Mouser and gave her a scratch behind the ears. "Okay, so M'lady, would you prefer salmon or salmon?"

Mouser meowed.

"Excellent choice." She popped open the lid and dished out the meat into a bowl. Mouser quickly pounced on it, ignoring the dry food in the timer tray next to it.

In the meantime, Hope had pulled back a kitchen chair and sat down, her hands cradling her face.

"What's your take on this group? Did we make a mistake on this venture?"

Anne joined Hope at the table. She pulled a scrunchie from her pocket and pulled her tawny waves into a ball at the back of her head. "We normally wouldn't have people that know each other like this, or if they do, they would actually be friends. I'm really thinking someone has an agenda here."

wouldn't have people that know each other like this, or if they do, they would actually be friends. I'm really thinking someone has an agenda here."

"I get the same impression. But who? And what?" Hope clasped her hands in front of her on the table.

"I don't know. But take a look at this." She pulled the crumpled paper out of her pocket.

"Whoa. Where did you find this?" Hope handed the note back to Anne.

"I was doing a quick room pass and turndown. I found it on the floor next to the wastepaper basket in the Nelsons' room. The question is, who's the intended recipient?"

Hope put her hand under her chin and replied, "Good question. If it was intended for the *Doctor*"—she quoted his name with her fingers in the air—"then it could be any of the three, though I don't really see Taylor writing a note. She'd tell you straight to your face."

"You're right there. No beating around the bush with her." Anne chuckled. "But I like her. What you see is what you get, at least I think so."

"Plus, what would be her reason for writing it? And we still haven't figured out if it was intended for the doc or his wife."

"I can't see Lil writing it either. She seems too—"

"Nice?" Hope replied.

"Yes, that's it. Proper."

"True, but with her there's the motive of Beth stealing her guy. And you know what they say about those quiet types."

"What's that?" Anne massaged her temples. A dull headache was coming on.

"They're always the ones you need to watch out for."

"Okay, so we both agree that we can't see Taylor writing a note like that. Lil could because she's nice, and according to you nice people are scary people."

"Could be. She reminds me of someone who doesn't like to make waves. But sometimes those type of people are more passive-aggressive in their actions. She could have decided to come simply to irritate the doc for dumping her, and to get under Beth's skin too."

"Well, I guess that could be the case. Then you think Lil sent it to Dr. Nelson? Or was the message intended for Beth?" Anne rubbed her eyes.

"It's possible, but it doesn't feel right," Hope replied.

"Agree again. That leaves Liz. She's always trying to make things better for Beth. Maybe she wrote him the note." Anne rested her chin on her hands and sighed. "Yet, I think Liz is like Taylor in that she'd say things straight to his face. She seems like someone that meets things head on."

"Agreed." Hope cocked her head. "I guess she could have, but why wait until they came here? Look how she called the doc out about smoking and how it made Beth feel."

"Ugh. I don't know." Anne ran her fingers through her hair, dislodging the scrunchy. She set to pulling her hair back up in a bun again.

Hope moaned. "All I do know is that we have a walk tomorrow morning with five people that seem to have all kinds of issues going on between them. I just thought it'd be a nice healthy way to start the morning."

"That's what you get for thinking." Anne smirked.

Hope stuck out her tongue. "Other than the walk and breakfast, maybe the classes will have enough distraction that the women won't have time to pull out the claws on one another."

Just then Kandi came through the back door. She pouted. "How come you guys didn't invite me over?"

Anne motioned to Kandi to join them. "You know you never need an invite. I just needed to talk with Hope about a note I found in the Nelsons' room."

"What note?"

Anne showed Kandi the note.

"That's not very nice." She thrust the note down as if it was a personal threat to her.

"No, kidding. We're trying to figure out if it was Taylor, Lil, or Liz who sent the note."

"But didn't you say you found it in the Nelsons' room?" Kandi's brow crinkled.

"Yes. So?" Anne motioned for Kandi to expound on her question.

"I'm just wondering why you think it's Taylor, Lil, or Liz."

Hope took up the questioning. "What do you mean?"

"If it was in their room, then wouldn't it make sense that either Dr. Nelson wrote it to Beth or she wrote it to him?"

Hope and Anne stared at one another. It had never occurred to them that Beth or Edward had written the note. Even more, was the other spouse the intended recipient or had the note been written for someone else and then discarded?

"That's a whole new way to look at it. Then we have to figure out if it was

Beth who wrote the note to give to him or the other way around?" Anne tapped her fingers on her chin.

"Or how about this? What if Beth had written the note to Lil and changed her mind?" said Hope.

"You did say, *like,* it was by the wastebasket. Maybe she wrote it but decided against it?"

"That's a good question, Kandi. Certainly, another way of looking at it that I

hadn't thought of."

"Geez. Too many questions and not enough answers. It's making my brain hurt." Anne cradled her cheeks on her hands.

"I'm going home now so I can get some sleep. Love ya." Kandi hugged Anne and Hope and then took her leave out the back door.

Hope stood and stretched. "Better get back over there and catch some z's before morning."

"See you then." Anne stood. "Hey, also, could you get Stewart to have another look around the place tomorrow? I'm used to my old house making settling noises, but those noises in the Inn have been pretty loud."

Hope hugged Anne. "I will. I've heard a few noises like that too. I thought I was just imagining it. I'll call Stewart and have him stop by while we're out on our walk."

"Get Kandi to do it." Anne teased, releasing Hope from the hug.

"Now Anne, if I didn't know better, I'd believe someone was trying to play matchmaker here."

"Moi?" Anne faked indignation.

Hope laughed and walked out the back door. Anne locked it and with Mouser tailing behind her, headed upstairs to the new master bedroom. Anne had enjoyed decorating it with an English country style and a color palette of soft peach and sage green. Over by the windows, she'd added in a lovely seating area where she could read or make plans for the day. She showered quickly and made her way to bed.

As she switched off the light on the small table next to the window, she looked outside. The stand of lilacs dividing the yard were only bare sticks. As she looked closer, a gasp sprang from her lips.

A large brown animal jumped up and bounded out of sight.

Chapter Seven

Morning came too early for Anne. She dragged the brush through her hair and slathered some lotion on her face. The extent of her makeup was some lip gloss. She looked at herself in the mirror repeating aloud, "Today is going to be a great day. Today is going to be a great day." *Oh please, let it be a great day.*

She longed for another cup of coffee but knew it wouldn't be smart to drink the dehydrating beverage before hitting the trail. Grabbing her soft alpaca wool hat that brought out the color in her hazel eyes, she headed for the door. On the kitchen counter, the water bottle stood full and ready; her gloves next to it. She fed Mouser, who not surprisingly opted for salmon again, and closed up the house before heading next door.

Steeling herself for the morning, she took the back kitchen steps and heard laughter coming from inside. That's got to be a good sign. Opening the door, Anne found Taylor chatting with Kandi and the two were chuckling about some private joke.

Lil stood in the doorway, not entirely in or out, looking not unlike a skittish cat that wants to have a quick exit in case of attack.

"Good morning, Anne," Lil spoke with her lilting, soft voice. "I hope you slept well."

Yep, proper had been the right description. "Yes, I did. Thanks for asking. How about you? Sleep well?" Anne stepped closer to the woman who was about Anne's height of five foot four.

"Yes, the bed was very comfortable. I really appreciate all the details taken here. When I first went into the room, I couldn't figure out the embroidery on the pillowcases. I knew they weren't the Inn's name. The F, S, M on each case is brilliant."

Taylor joined, and the pair and Kandi went back to breakfast prep. "F, S, M?"

"Did you see the initials on the pillowcases? I believe they stand for firm, soft, and medium. Am I correct, Anne?"

Anne gave her a thumbs-up. "Spot-on."

Taylor let out a hearty chuckle. "I was so tired that I just grabbed whatever pillow I landed on. I guess it worked, but I was asleep, so who knows!"

They all laughed. Anne really liked Taylor's jocularity.

"Hey, who decided on a party and didn't invite me?" Liz feigned indignation.

"You're certainly invited to any party in this house, Liz. Did you sleep well?" Anne took the cup Liz had been holding. "I did, but something woke me. I thought I heard footsteps. I figured it was someone going down to the kitchen for a midnight snack or something. But they didn't seem to be in the hall or on the main stairs."

"I heard it too," Lil spoke up.

Taylor responded, "I didn't hear anything. But I pretty much fall deep asleep once my head hits the pillow."

"We'll check into it. Thanks for letting us know. Now if everyone's ready, we should get going. Anyone seen Dr. and Mrs. Nelson?"

A gruff voice answered back, "We're coming."

The pair entered the room and Beth sighed deeply.

She evidently doesn't want to do this so why come? Did she feel the need to keep a tight leash on the doctor?

Liz went over to Beth and spoke to her friend while Edward strode over to Kandi. "Hey there, got anything I might like over here?" He reached out toward Kandi who deftly moved out from under his arm. "I'm working on the breakfast for when you return but you'll have some snacks on the trail. Would you like a piece of fruit or some nuts, sir?"

That guy gives me the creeps. He's too charming. Smarmy.

He shook his head to the negative. "I'm going out back and I'll wait for you there."

Ahhh, needs his morning nicotine hit most likely.

He walked outside. As everyone else shrugged into coats and hats, Hope came over and handed Anne a backpack. She put it on, and the group trudged out into the crisp morning air. Anne glimpsed at the thermometer as she headed out the door. Thirty-six. Perfect. It was so funny how the low humidity made things feel so much warmer in Colorado. She figured people would be shedding jackets on the way back. They caught up to Edward who stuck the vape pen into his pocket as the ladies exited the kitchen.

Before she left, Anne popped over to Kandi. "Hey, sweetie. All good on the stove front?"

"Yes, I've got everything pretty much ready and timed out, so things should be ready to eat when you return. I also called Stewart to come over and see about that noise. He said he'll try to swing by later."

"Great. I better get out there before they leave without me." They kissed each other on the cheek and Anne hurried down the stairs to the gazebo where Hope was giving some instruction to the group.

Heads nodded as she explained about altitude sickness, drinking water in the bottles they had been given, and going at their own pace. Hope set out toward a clearing between the trees that led them to the trailhead. Reaching the dirt track, Edward took up lead position moving ahead of Hope. Liz and Beth followed a few feet behind him, and Taylor and Lil walked a bit farther behind. Anne took up the rear. The patches of snow still evident in the trees along the lane helped reflect some light, but they had been wise to bring headlamps.

As happens during walks, people settled into a comfortable speed and moved around, with Taylor striking up a conversation with Liz. Edward had slowed his pace, and Lil had fallen back with Hope who had joined Anne at the rear. Hope rolled her eyes at Anne but made her way over to walk with Edward.

"So, Lil, you all went to college together?" Anne hoped her question would be a neutral topic.

"Yes. We all came from the north—Beth from New York, Liz and I from the Boston area, and Taylor from Texas."

Anne noted how Lil had left Edward out of the group. "And you were all wanting to be doctors or in the medical field?"

"Only two of us wanted to be doctors—me and
. . . Edward. I think Liz was there because her father was
a doctor and her mother a hospital administrator. Of all
of us, I think Liz is the best at seeing a vision and going
for it. I think she ended up in administration over some
assisted-living facilities.

"Taylor wanted to do something to help people—
she just hates seeing people in misery, so she became of
all things, a palliative nurse. I couldn't do that, but she
has the calling, I guess. Lots of her patients have died
peacefully in their sleep and didn't need to transition into
hospice care. She's so great with the families. I think of
all of us, she picked the route that really suits her
personality. She's a very caring person. I'm glad we've
remained friends, even with the distance between us,"
said Lil.

Hmmm, was there a reason she hadn't included
Beth? Best to keep on a neutral subject.

"And Edward chose to become a cardiologist."

Lil replied, "Yes, an interesting choice, given his
heart problems."

Anne couldn't help but wonder if there was a bit of
double entendre in Lil's statement. "Forgive me for
overstepping, but it seems like Edward is the reason for
some of the angst we saw yesterday."

"I blame myself really," Lil responded, which
surprised Anne. "I should have left school when
everything happened, but I was so enamored with
everything I was learning. I had no idea things would
turn out as they did."

Anne really wanted to delve deeper, but she knew it
wasn't the time or the place. Maybe she could ask Taylor
about Lil's statement later.

"Did you become a doctor?" Anne pulled off her gloves and stuck them in her pocket. She shrugged out of the microfiber jacket and tied it around her waist. Lil did the same, but as Lil pulled her coat off, her sleeve rode up, and Anne saw a nasty scar on Lil's wrist. Noticing Anne staring, Lil pulled the sleeve down.

"To answer your question, yes, I got my degree. I changed colleges and went into pharmaceutical studies. I attended Oxford and then when I returned to the states, I majored in cardiac pharmacology."

Edward and Lil had both been focused on cardiac studies. Had Lil been trying to get away from the heartbreak by changing schools?

"Hey, you two, come on!" Hope was signaling with her arm. "Hurry!" Anne and Lil sprinted up to the group who stood facing the forest with the lake beyond. Anne squinted, trying to see what Hope was so excited about when a giant creature raised its head from out of a boggy area next to the lake.

Taylor whispered excitedly, "A moose! A moose!"

Anne watched the majestic creature with the rest of the group, each entranced by the sight in front of them. As it moved off into the dense forest, the group collectively released its breath.

"That was amazing." Beth turned to Edward, who had somehow ended up next to Lil.

Hope quickly realized the need to get moving, so she said, "Ladies, Doctor. Just a bit farther and we have another treat for you."

Hope's words seem to break the spell. Edward moved quickly away from Lil who did the same thing. It was like an unseen gravitational pull had drawn them together, only for them to wake up to its reality as they found themselves standing side by side.

Taylor quipped, "It'll be hard to beat what we just saw." She stamped ahead and waved her arm behind her. "Come on, ya'll. Time's a-wasting."

Edward and Beth walked together with Lil and Liz in the second group. Taylor hung back with Anne.

"Whoa. That could have turned out really badly." She chuckled under her breath. If Taylor had seen what happened, who else had noticed it? Anne said nothing but was glad that no argument had ensued.

They reached the curve where Beth sat on a big rock. Anne had perched on that same outcropping not so very long ago, and it sent a small shiver down her spine, like a dark omen. Hope stopped and faced the group. "Not much farther, and we'll take a break before we head back. Our friend Eliza, who's out of town on a modeling assignment, said to feel free to use her deck. As we go around the corner, you'll see a set of stairs, and that's where we're heading."

The group followed Hope up to the deck where they were greeted with the beautiful rays of sunlight over the lake. Anne opened her backpack while Hope did the same. Hope poured hot tea while Anne passed out a combination of savory and sweet pastries. Everyone sat in silence, enjoying the view and the hot drinks.

When Beth and Lil noted the need for a bathroom break, Anne walked them down and opened the guest bathroom door on the lower floor. As the group descended the stairs back to the trail, Anne waited for the pair. She heard low voices coming from inside the door.

"You had your chance. Now back off." Beth's voice was low and menacing.

"Why? You don't love him. You never have. All you wanted was what he could give you." Lil's strong retort surprised Anne. *Was the woman's appearance and mannerisms only a front? And what about the scar on her arm?*

Lil continued, "The only reason you were in medical school was to marry a doctor. All of us knew it. We laughed at you behind your back."

"Why you little—"

Whoa. Anne needed to get in their quick but as she moved toward the door, Lil appeared. Her face was tinged a bright pink. She spotted Anne and dropped her eyes. She had evidently not expected to be overheard.

Anne heard footsteps and quickly moved away from the door. Beth appeared in the door, hands tightly clenched and the hate on her face blatant.

"Beth, I don't think we've had much chance to get acquainted. How about walking with me for a bit?" Anne knew she needed to defuse this situation quickly.

The conversation within the group became more subdued on the walk back to the Inn. Anne did notice that Dr. Nelson and Liz had gone first and moved far ahead of the group. The pair appeared to be in an intense conversation. Occasionally Liz would turn back and look to see the group behind them.

Is Liz making sure they aren't getting too far ahead of us or that they're far enough ahead that they aren't overheard?

Back at the house, Kandi had prepared a fantastic breakfast, and, after changing of shoes and outfits, the banter around the table over Kandi's culinary skills gave Anne hope that the day would continue without any significant incidents.

"Hello, Hello!" Marie's voice carried into the room. Anne led her into the dining room where Hope took on the task of introducing her to the group. Edward had excused himself after eating.

"Ladies, this is Marie, and she's going to be helping with our lessons on tinctures, tisanes, and tonics." Hope motioned to Marie who gave a small wave to the group.

Hope continued, "I'll be talking about elderberry as one of the herbs, and she has offered to show us how to make her award-winning elderberry cordial. We'll talk a lot about using food as medicine to prevent colds and flu which tend to spike during the winter months. We'll take a short break to get things set up in the kitchen, and we'll start the class at ten. This gives you some free time before we start. Any questions?"

All the women shook their heads. Beth and Liz headed upstairs together. Taylor went off with Kandi to her house to get her savory pastry recipe and to see Kandi's chicken coop. Lil exited the door to the portico.

As Hope cleared the breakfast dishes from the table, Anne began rinsing the plates. As Anne glanced out the window, she saw Lil down by the area marked for the new cutting garden. As she watched, Anne spied the doctor leave the shade of the gazebo, a puff of quick vapor revealing why he was there.

Edward glanced back up at the house and then walked over to where Lil stood. Anne knew that Beth wouldn't be able to see Lil and her husband from the window in her room. He came over and stood next to Lil. The woman looked up at him, and Anne could see the sadness in her face. His face echoed hers, but where hers held longing, his also showed longing. He spoke some words to her, but she ducked her head, shaking it. He grabbed both of her arms, but she pulled free from him and ran back toward the house.

Had he been telling her he was sorry? What had happened to cause him to choose Beth over Lil? Had Beth seen her chance when Lil went to Oxford?

Anne finished loading the dishwasher and set to wiping down the counters when she spied Liz sprinting toward the gazebo. Liz turned back to the house, but the morning sun meant that Liz couldn't see Anne through the kitchen windows. Anne could tell by the gestures that Liz and Edward were having an argument. Liz was giving him a piece of her mind. *Had she seen him talking to Lil? Was she taking up for Beth, yet once again?*

Finally, Liz threw her hands up in the air and strode off toward the driveway. Anne opened the window a bit to let in some fresh Colorado air. Then she emptied the trash and walked out to the can by the garage. As she started to move back toward the house, Anne watched as Taylor advanced across the yard from Kandi's house. Taylor must have watched the entire episode with Lil or Liz because she headed over to where Dr. Nelson sat in the gazebo puffing on the vape pen. He looked up at her from his seat but said nothing as Taylor loudly launched into some choice words that weren't fit for public consumption. He jumped up from his seat, said something Anne couldn't make out, and shook his fist at her. Taylor grabbed the vape pen and shoved it into his chest.

Yikes. The quicker Dr. Nelson was gone, the better.

Anne would later regret that choice of words.

Chapter Eight

"Being a snoop again, Anne?" She jumped at Hope's words.

"Who needs to be a snoop? It's like watching reality television right outside your window but without sound. I need the remote!"

Hope laughed. "I prefer the mute button about now! I've never seen such a mess as this group."

"I think it's all due to that guy out there." She tipped her head to where Edward sat.

"Whoever or whatever, I'm hoping today gets better. I'm not enjoying this enterprise thus far."

"I hear ya. I just think we got the worst guests possible for the launch. After this it should be smooth sailing." Anne hung the dishcloth on a hook under the sink.

"We can hope."

Anne crossed her arms. "Since everyone's upstairs,

anything we need to get done to prepare?"

"Yes. Would you mind taking me over to the shop? I'd like to check in on mom and see how Autumn's getting along with everything."

"We've got time. I may run over to the pet store while you do that. I need to get a glove for Mouser's fur. The other one isn't working out." Anne picked at cat hair on her sweater.

Hope laughed. "I was going to ask if that was a cat-hair sweater."

"Ha. Ha. You're so funny." She sighed. "I do love Mouser to pieces, but I think all my clothing is a magnet for her." She wiped down her arms and then pushed up her sleeves. The day was already warming up. Anne continued, "Let me just call Kandi so she will know we'll be out for a bit. I don't want to leave that crew alone too long. I'd hate to come back to a massacre."

After connecting with Kandi, who came back to the Inn, Anne and Hope drove into town. Anne parked her newer blue Dodge 4x4 on the street. As Hope walked into her shop, Anne strolled down to Patty's Pampered Pets.

The bell over the door sounded and a woman in her thirties appeared from behind the counter. "Hi Anne. How's poor lonely Mouser?"

"Ha ha. Not biting, Pat." While the shop owner's name was actually Patricia, she went by Pat or Patty. She also volunteered at the local animal rescue and was always trying to get people to adopt or foster animals.

"Ah, come on. Doesn't he need a friend?"

"I'm his friend." She looked at a collection of squeaky toys. *Well, maybe just one of these.* She grabbed a bright orange ball from the basket.

The bell rang again and a teenager in a dark hoodie

came in. "Need any help?" Pat called out.

The teen shook his head and stuffed his hands in his pockets.

Something about the boy niggled at the back of Anne's mind. She grabbed some more treats for Mouser and went to the counter where she set the items down. "I'm looking for one of those gloves that comb fur. Got anything like that?"

"Sure." She came out from around the counter and walked toward an aisle with all sorts of grooming gadgets with names like "fur terminator."

As Anne tried to figure out which glove she wanted, the teen had plodded up to the cash register. In his left arm he held a bag of dry dog food and a bag of jerky treats. She heard Pat speak. "Hey, Spence, haven't seen you in a while."

He kept his head down. "Been busy."

He pulled out a pile of crumpled bills and set them on the counter. As Pat began counting out the money, he emptied his jacket pocket of spare change.

"Just a bit short, but no worries. You can make it up by helping out in the stockroom this weekend if that works for you." She rang up the purchase.

"Will I get more if I work more?"

"Sure. I could definitely use more help after school and on the weekends. Want to dress up as a pirate and work the front, helping people?"

He mumbled, "No."

Pat had capitalized on the wearing of an eyepatch when she'd opened the pet store by wearing a pirate costume last October. What the kids who now called her Pirate Patty didn't know was that she'd had eye surgery due to a fall while skiing. Now afternoons and on Saturdays, she would transform into Pirate Patty. The kids loved it, as she would often read stories she borrowed from Sorcha at the bookstore and have one of the pets needing adoption from the shelter next to her. Parents said Patty didn't play fair as it was rare for an animal not to be adopted on those weekends.

"Okay, fine. I can still use help in the back too." She put the jerky into a bag. "Still feeding strays, huh." She motioned to the dog food.

"Yeah."

"Oh, I forgot to tell you that you were right about that website tweak. I've seen a lot more hits and sales have been steadily increasing online. That'll be really good come winter when business really slows down. I'll still be able to place orders and let the delivery service take care of it for me." Pat smiled. "Moving here was the best thing I ever did. I can make money while I'm out skiing. Is there anything better than that?"

Anne who had taken more falls than she could count while skiing, and now stuck to snow-shoeing, stood behind Spencer and said nothing.

Spencer straightened a bit, but still kept his head down.

Anne coughed, and he swiveled toward her. That's where she knew him. He was the kid she'd seen at the police station last year during the time she was visiting Kandi.

He grabbed the dog food tighter and headed toward the entrance. As he exited, Anne saw Hope headed inside. It looked like the pair were having words. Anne moved toward the storefront and opened the door.

Hope's voice was louder than normal. "Do you know you could have been killed?" Hope had grabbed his forearm as the boy shook it off. "You don't run out in front of cars like that—especially at night."

"So, he's—" Anne jumped in.

"Yes. He's the boy we saw the other night out in the cul-de-sac."

Anne faced him. "What were you doing—"

The boy turned and ran across the street. A truck's horn sounded as he raced across the other lane. He dropped the bag of dog food, but quickly retrieved it before looking behind him to see if anyone had followed. Anne and Hope watched as he disappeared behind a tree before spotting him turn toward the trail that connected the town with the wilderness area.

"Kids!" Anne and Hope said at the same time.

After Anne had paid Pat for her items, they walked over to the truck. A voice called out. "Hope! Wait, Hope!" A young woman in her early twenties with a multi-colored scarf covering her dreadlocks jogged over to them. She clutched at her knees while catching her breath. "This altitude is killer."

"Anne, meet Autumn. Autumn, this is Anne."

"Hi." She stood up and Anne gazed into warm deep-brown eyes. She wore an apron over a white linen tunic and baggy, green khaki-colored pants.

"Hi." Anne shook the young woman's hand.

She turned to Hope. "I just talked with Missy and she can hang out with Miss Faith if I need to bring anything over to the Inn."

Faith was Hope's mother. Her periods of lucidity varied, and she needed someone close by in case she decided to wander away from her apartment.

"Great."

"Nice meeting you, Anne. Got to run." Without waiting for a reply, Autumn turned and ambled back down the alley.

"I need her energy."

CORDIAL KILLING

Hope responded, "You and me both. She's eager to learn and has been a big help with the herbal preparations." She glanced at her watch. "We better get back to the Inn. Marie's probably ready to get started."

"Oh geez. Totally forgot. Kandi's probably ready to kill us."

Chapter Nine

The ladies were all chatting among themselves when Marie began. Anne watched as Marie, a portly woman with a ruddy complexion, reveled in the spotlight. Hope had let it be known that Marie sought out gossip like a cat sought a mouse, so Anne should beware of what she shared with the woman. Since that time, Anne had steered clear of any conversation that went beyond the weather or other generalities.

Marie held up the glass decanter and smiled widely. Inside, the elderberry liquid glimmered like a ruby jewel. "This is my award-winning elderberry cordial."

Anne chimed in, "Five years running." She held up her right hand, stretching out her five fingers. Marie beamed at the praise offered.

"Well, yes, that's true. And today is your lucky day, ladies, because I'm going to be sharing my recipe with you. We'll make the cordial, which is a fairly quick process. You'll be able to take that home with you to let it finish the process. Tonight, at dinner, you'll get to sample my cordial." She set the decanter down on the table.

Hope moved over and stood next to Marie. In comparison to Marie's short stature, Hope was a tall, thin woman who presented herself in such a caring manner that people instantly trusted her. Over the course of the partnership on the bed and breakfast, Hope had grown beyond being Anne's doctor and herbalist. She had become a dear and trusted friend.

Hope was answering a question about the day's schedule, "Once the cordial is done, we'll begin talking about great medicinal plants, just like elderberry, to add to your garden."

"Liz has the most beautiful garden," Beth interjected, "She's got all kinds of flowers—spring-flowering tulips, hyacinths, foxglove, and in the summer, her dahlias—"

Liz flinched and looked up at the group. "Now Beth, you have the same flowers in your garden." She playfully nudged her friend.

"Thanks to you." Beth squeezed Liz's arm.

Anne noticed a shadow pass over Liz's face. She looked at the two women. Did Beth take advantage of her friendship with Liz? Or was Liz the type of friend that wanted to mother her friend and didn't mind playing that role for her? She'd been at Beth's side whenever Dr. Nelson had made his insults toward Beth or women in general. Or was she just someone that didn't like being put on the spot in front of others?

"I love flowers," Lil spoke, and it caused everyone to turn since she so seldom spoke up.

"I remember." Beth looked at Lil. "Remember that

time we stole into Taylor's room and put smiley face notes all over her room. Taylor had broken up with some boy. You never did tell us—"

Taylor jerked up from her chair. "Is there time for a potty break before we get started? All that coffee, you know."

Anne also rose. "Of course. Everyone if you'd like to take a break, you can help yourself to more coffee or tea and then we'll get started."

Beth laughed. "We were all so young and naïve back then."

"Some of us more than others," Taylor said under her breath as she left the room.

Liz got up and went to the sideboard, adding more coffee to her cup. She raised the pot, signaling if anyone else wanted a refill.

"I wish we had more pictures from that time," Beth said. "Of course, we have our more formal ones in our scrubs, but not just us hanging out."

"If I recall," interjected Liz, "that was because Taylor said she'd put on the freshman fifteen and she didn't want her picture taken until she'd lost the weight."

"Yes, now that you said that, I do remember her wearing that really big, oversized scrub. I always teased her about it, but she said it helped her move better. But she couldn't fool me."

"I bet she did," Lil said under her breath.

"Excuse me?" Beth responded, and Liz turned to face toward Lil.

"I said I bet she did like wearing it looser to work easier. They could get twisted pretty easily."

Taylor had returned and stood in the doorway. She looked pointedly at Lil but said nothing.

Anne watched as something—a bit of sadness

perhaps—passed between the two women.

"Ladies, everyone ready?" Marie motioned everyone to the kitchen where the ingredients and quart-sized jars stood.

As everyone filed into the kitchen, Kandi looked up from what looked like a list. "Good morning, everyone. You all sleep well?"

Affirmative answers passed around. Taylor said, "Kandi, I forgot to tell you earlier, that stuffed French toast was out of this world."

The others nodded.

"I'm glad you liked it." Kandi beamed. "I like experimenting in the kitchen, and when I saw the ingredients for the cordial, I thought, *like,* why not?"

Marie asked, "What kind was it?"

"I made cheese stuffed French toast with orange rind, coated with a cinnamon honey mixture and topped with elderberry syrup."

"It was delicious," Taylor replied. "Do you have your recipes in a cookbook? I'd like to buy one."

Kandi blushed and turned to Anne. "Well, no. *Like* I never, *like,* thought—"

"That's a great idea, Taylor. As you note, Kandi is an excellent cook." Anne beamed at Kandi. "Maybe that's something we can work on doing and having on offer for future guests. But for now, we'd be happy to supply you with the recipes from this weekend. Hope, I'll pop out with Kandi for a minute and then I'll be back in to help."

Anne and Kandi walked into the office. Anne shut the door behind her and then grabbed Kandi in a hug. "I'm so proud of you. I knew you had the natural talent of a chef."

"I'm, *like,* so overwhelmed." Kandi wiped a happy

tear from her eye before sinking down in the chair opposite the desk. "I never thought people would be that interested. I just hoped they'd like my food."

"They don't just like your food, they love your food! And what's not to love? You cook it wonderfully while adding your own uniqueness to it, and you present it beautifully on the plate."

Anne moved around to the other side of the two-person desk and sat down on the yoga ball. When Hope had first brought one, Anne hadn't been so sure about it. But once Hope had added the chair support, she had quickly sold Anne on it. She scooted forward.

"I think this could be a great addition to what we offer. Although, it's not like you need more money or anything." Anne grinned at Kandi.

Kandi had inherited millions from her late mother, but it hadn't changed the young woman at all. Instead, she'd hired a good lawyer who had put everything in a trust, and she now would have a very comfortable living for the rest of her life. She'd purchased some property in and around town so was thrilled to be a part of updating Ralph's old Victorian into a bed and breakfast. While Hope kept her practice, these occasional weekend workshops would also help finance the round-the-clock care that her mother, Faith, now required.

Kandi bit the inside of her lip signaling that she wanted to share something but wasn't sure if she should.

"Okay, I can see that something's on your mind. Spill the beans, young lady." Anne clasped her hands together on the desk.

Kandi moved her chair closer to the desk and lowered her voice. "I think one of them may be a thief."

"What!" Anne hadn't been expecting that.

"I don't mean, *like*, in a major way. But I know I had

exactly what I needed for lunch and dinner tonight. Now I get that some people may want a snack, so I had in a bit extra, but I've noticed food going missing. Yesterday it was some of the pastries I'd made for the walk. I'd wanted to make a batch to see how long before they got cold. This morning when I was making breakfast, I noticed some of the bread, cheese, and roast beef missing. I don't mind them making a snack, but they didn't even close the stuff up. They can't have been in that much of a hurry."

She continued, "So now I've got to run into town to the store because some of the items I had planned to use for dinner are also gone. Plus, lots of the snack foods—chips, cookies." She shrugged her shoulders. "I just thought I should, *like*, tell you."

"Yes, thanks for telling me this, Kandi. We will need to sit down with Hope and figure this out for the future. I'm with you that I don't mind the guests fixing a snack, but we need to have some guidelines or something. Maybe a small refrigerator upstairs and locking the main kitchen at night," Anne said, more to herself than to Kandi.

Kandi got up. "I'm going to go on to the store while everyone's in the kitchen." She headed for the door as Anne rose from her seat and stretched her back. "Oh, also, one of the headlamps is also missing."

Anne frowned at that. "They could have forgotten to drop it in the basket on the way back in this morning. I'll ask them about it."

Anne walked to the remodeled kitchen. It had been dark and cramped before, but the removal of the wall between the butler's pantry and the kitchen had made it into a big, beautiful space. In the center of the room stood an attractive wood workstation that provided plenty of space for all to gather around it. She had to hand it to Stewart. He had taken her concept of a worktable and made it even better by creating storage in the middle, and places for stools all around it.

Marie was pointing out the original shelving which now held jars of dried herbs and a combination of brown and blue bottles. "This is where you'll put your cordial once you're done." She opened a cabinet and pointed.

A small grin appeared on Anne's face as she noticed how the women had all taken the same positions from when they sat in the dining room. It was funny how people were creatures of habit. They had all chosen the same seating arrangement. It was an idiosyncrasy she had seen more than once in her life.

Beth and Liz sat on the left with the chair that Marie had vacated. On the right side sat Taylor and Anne who joined them in the last seat. Hope now occupied what would be considered the head of the table. She rose.

"Okay, everyone. Normally we'd take this time to introduce ourselves but seeing as you all know each other, how about if someone from the group shares how you first met." She sat back down on her stool and waited.

"I'll do it," Beth replied cheerfully.

Anne couldn't help but notice the massive change from this morning's outburst. *Hmmm, I wonder if she couldn't use some of Hope's hormonal tea too.* She giggled to herself.

"It was our first day of class," she said, "and the professor called out 'Elizabeth.' All of us said 'Here!' at the same time."

Liz took up the story. "Since there were others with the same last name as some of us, the professor would have the same issue, so he asked if we'd come up with nicknames or a way for him to distinguish us from one another."

"This was back before current technology, so there was no checking in that way," Taylor interjected.

Anne piped up. "That makes sense. But what about you, Taylor?"

"Yep. Odd man out." She grinned. "I was rooming with Lil, and so she invited everyone over to our dorm to talk about it."

Beth continued the story. "I think a television was on and a commercial came on. It was Elizabeth Taylor on some old commercial about some perfume."

"White Diamonds," Lil replied.

Liz joined in, "My mom always asked for that perfume for Christmas. I think the perfume came out in the late nineties. But they played that ad a lot over the years. I think I was around eight or nine the time I saw it, but my mom always pointed the commercial out to my dad, so I guess it stuck in my memory." Liz laughed. "It's funny what you remember."

Anne nodded her head. "That commercial was on for decades."

"Yes. It ran for years until 2017." Taylor nodded. "Anyway, that's when Liz had started laughing because we realized we were Elizabeth and Taylor."

Marie turned to Taylor. "You're very sure of yourself."

Anne shot Hope a glance. The last thing they needed was Marie irritating their guests.

"I am," Taylor replied, "I read it one time."

"You read it?" Marie inquired.

"Yes. I have a pretty good memory. Once it's in here"—she pointed to her head—"it sticks."

Liz said, "That's true. You don't want to get on

Taylor's bad side. She has a long memory."

"I'm still upset you broke my favorite cup with the horses on it," Taylor quipped.

"See!" Liz pointed at Taylor. "Grudge-holder."

"Cup-breaker."

Liz stuck her tongue out at Taylor.

Taylor held up her hands and turned back to the story. "Actually, as you know, my last name is Taylor and my first name is Christie. But in some ways, college was a bit like the military and people were often called by their last name, so it just stuck." She shrugged her shoulders. "Before we knew it we were known as Elizabeth and Taylor. Kind of a joke around campus, but all in good fun."

"Those were such fun times," Beth said, and the others nodded.

"So how did you and Anne meet, Hope?" Lil motioned to where Anne sat.

Hope looked at Anne, and Anne spoke, "When I first arrived, Hope helped me with some hormonal issues. It made a huge difference."

Hope winked at Anne. Much better to give that reason than say that Anne had found her father dead in his compost pile out back. When they started fixing up Ralph's house and property to turn it into the Brandywine Inn, one of the first things they did was put in a water feature where the compost pile had been situated. Unknown to anyone but them, they also put in a memorial stone with etching to honor Ralph. You had to know it was there, as the memorial faced away from the house. They had added the gazebo close by so people could take in the heady lilac smell when they were in bloom.

"Hope, you want to get us started?" Anne passed

out notebooks to each lady.

"Let's start with the differences between a tincture, tisane, and tonic, ladies. An herbal tincture is a medicinal liquid often made by adding herbs to alcohol or, for a child's preparation, glycerin can be substituted. On the other hand, a tisane is often referred to as a medicinal tea which is steeped for a short time, unlike an infusion which may be steeped overnight to pull the beneficial medicinal constituents from the roots and other parts of plants. Finally, a tonic is a medicinal drink that is often used to promote wellness, like Marie's cordial. Over the weekend we'll learn about and partake in all of these. For now, I'll hand it over to Marie. Take it away, Marie." Hope sat down, and Marie moved to the head of the table.

"Ladies, as you can see, we have the ingredients lined up in front of you. For this class and due to the season, we're using dried elderberries. For your canning jar, I prefer wide-mouth—"

Anne shot Hope a look, and they both tried to hide their smirks with their hands. Only something that the town's snoop and gossip would say could elicit that response. Hope coughed to mask the noise of Anne's giggling.

Marie looked up.

"Sorry, I apologize. Anne's not being serious, and it's a private joke from earlier," Hope announced to the group.

Anne wadded up a napkin and threw it at Hope. "We'll behave now."

Marie continued, "As I was saying, these are the jars I like to use for the cordial. The most important rule is always to label your jars. You always say that you'll remember and come back and label them later, but trust me, you won't. That's why labeling is one of the most important habits to get into doing first thing." She picked up a roll of masking tape and some black sharpies. "If everyone will write your name, the date, and the title, 'elderberry cordial' and tape to your bottle."

Anne glanced over at Hope. Maybe this could help them figure out who wrote the note.

Marie poured some elderberries into a glass measuring cup. "For dried elderberries, you'll need one and one-quarter cups." Everyone poured the berries into their measuring cups and raised them, waiting for the next command. When Marie poured hers into her jar, they all followed suit.

"If you use fresh berries, use two cups."

Taylor made a note on a pad.

"Don't worry, I'll provide the complete recipe for when you leave so you won't have to take notes now."

Hope said, "Elderberries are great for the body's immune system and help with the prevention of colds and flu."

"If you don't mind my saying so," Beth interjected, "I'm surprised you gave up medicine for herbalism. I'd think that traditional medicine would be more profitable."

Anne saw Hope bristle a bit, but Hope was calm when she responded. "Technically, I didn't give up allopathic medicine, but I wanted to focus more on prevention instead of treatment. I can still prescribe medicine or another course of treatment if I feel that it is in the best interest of the patient."

"I'm sorry, I didn't mean—"

"No offense taken. I moved back here to care for my mom. Being here in this town, with so many great people, is the best compensation I could ever wish for."

She smiled. "Plus, look at all you lovely ladies. You all have extensive medical backgrounds, and yet here you are learning about tinctures."

"Agreed," said Lil. "I studied—and continue to study—pharmaceutical drugs for years. I do believe they are of benefit, but I'm concerned with some of the contraindications and the serious side effects I'm seeing more often. I'm always wanting to learn about supplements and other items such as herbal remedies that interact with or complement allopathic medicine. I hope to apply for a research grant on the interactions between pharmaceutical methodologies and alternative treatments."

"True," said Hope. "For instance, some studies are noting that astragalus root tincture can work with chemotherapy treatment to help build immunity and ease nausea. The more we learn to focus on prevention and treat the body holistically, the better the result for any patient. Best of luck on getting the grant."

Marie loudly cleared her throat.

"Sorry." Hope raised her hands in the air. "Rabbit trail. My bad."

Marie had the ladies add one-quarter cup of rose hips while Hope spoke of their high vitamin C content. Each woman then took up a plane and grated orange peel.

"Now that you have the two tablespoons of peel, you'll need the same amount of minced ginger." She passed around a knob of fresh ginger. "When you're done, shake the ingredients to disperse them a bit, and then drop in your cinnamon stick." The ladies all followed her lead.

Marie pulled bottles of brandy from the sideboard. "This cordial uses brandy as its base. Hope will tell you that depending on the tincture, most are usually made with vodka or Everclear. Tonics or elixirs will often use alcohol or water. For children or those who can't have any alcohol, glycerin or an apple cider vinegar base is a good substitute. However, the alcohol helps to pull the medicinal components from the herbs and other ingredients, so that is why it is most commonly used."

She opened a bottle of brandy and poured three cups into a measuring container. "I like a touch of sweetness in my cordial, so I use some of Bill's honey. I prefer a local source, as the honey comes from local pollens and nectars. This is what will make your cordial unique to your area and the taste may vary because of it. You can also use maple syrup if you can't find any quality honey." She went to the counter and returned with a jar full of glistening, golden honey. "I would start with one-eighth to one-quarter cup of honey and if you want it sweeter, go up from there." She stirred the honey into the jar with a wooden spoon.

"All right, ladies." Marie placed her hands on the jar and raised it in the air. "You've just made your first batch of cordial. If you'll wipe off any spills and cover the tops, we'll be finished with this part."

Lil reached for a jar lid. "How long before it's ready?"

"You'll store it in a cool, dry place and it should be ready in about three to four weeks. Then you'll strain it and put it in a bottle of your choosing. If you make it in late October or early November, it makes a nice gift for the upcoming holiday season."

"Oh, that's a great idea," Taylor remarked as she stood and walked over to the cabinet.

Hope gathered up the measuring cups and Taylor helped her with another tray. From the kitchen, Anne heard Taylor call out, "Hey Beth, I thought Edward was going into Denver for the day."

Beth went to the window, and Anne looked over her shoulder toward where they could see Dr. Nelson sitting in a chair in the gazebo, his head slumped. "That man. Probably out smoking again and fell asleep."

She grabbed her sweater from her chair as Liz said, "I'll walk with you."

Anne began filling the sink with soapy water as she watched the two women head toward the gazebo. Beth bent down while touching Edward's arm. She jolted back up. As she stepped back, Liz crouched down by the man and put her fingers to his neck.

Oh no. That's can't be a good sign. "Hope, come here!" She called out and moved to the back door.

Liz sprinted toward the house as Anne and the others came running from inside. Liz yelled, "Edward's had a heart attack!"

As Marie rushed to the phone, the rest of the group ran out to the gazebo.

Anne reached Beth as Taylor bent over Dr. Nelson.

Taylor turned to the group. "No need for an ambulance. He's dead."

Chapter Ten

"I can't believe it. I can't believe it." Beth moved to his right side with Liz following. Liz reached for Beth, but Beth shook off her arm and turned away. Beth took a step back. There was a loud pop. Liz reached down to the ground where Beth had stepped. In her hand, Liz held up Edward's broken vape pen. Beth looked at it and said, "Oh, give me that. I wish Edward hadn't had that nasty habit." She stuck it in her pocket. She turned back to Edward and it was if an invisible force had connected with her. She gasped and covered her mouth with her hands.

Shock registered on her face as Beth allowed Liz's second attempt to embrace her. The two women clung to each other and stepped back and away from Edward's chair.

Tears had sprung to Lil's eyes.

Anne felt helpless. She shoved her hands into her

pockets, and her fingers hit on the crumpled note.

Now it's your turn to suffer.

It dawned on Anne that this could be a crime scene and they'd just trampled over everything. She moved into action. "Everyone, we need to move out of the gazebo. We'll need to allow some room for paramedics to get in there."

Marie had now joined the group and was bristling with excitement. If she told any of the women that this was the second death at the house, Anne would personally wring her neck.

Hope sidled up next to Anne and motioned for her to step away from the pack. When they had moved a few yards back, Hope whispered, "What do you think?"

"I'm not sure. Probably a heart attack. Dr. Nelson had serious heart issues and sounded like he switched his regular tobacco habit to the vape pen not too long ago. But—"

"The note, right?"

"Yes, that muddies the water. Plus, I have a bad feeling in my gut about all this. I'm not sure if the note was to Edward or to Beth, but it could be significant." She quieted her voice to ensure no one overheard. "I know that people can go into shock. But don't you think it's strange that Beth hasn't shed a tear?"

"That could be shock. We each grieve differently."

They heard the arrival of the ambulance in the driveway. Hope jogged over to the driveway to direct the group to the backyard. Another EMT accompanied Sheriff Carson, who had also arrived. Carson strode toward the group, his robust manner exerting his authority.

Hope and Anne walked over to the sheriff. He tipped his Stetson. "What do we have here?"

Hope nodded toward the gazebo. "Dr. Edward Nelson, one of our guests. His wife, Beth, is the lady with the streaked blonde hair. The woman with her arm around her is Beth's friend, Liz. Of course, you know Marie."

"Yes." He pulled out his pad and made notes of the names.

"The other two ladies are Taylor, the, um, taller lady, and Lil is the petite one. They're friends of the other ladies and attended college at the same time. When they first—"

"Just the facts, Ms. Freemont." He walked over to the group.

Anne mimicked, "Just the facts, Ms. Freemont."

Without attracting attention from the group of mourners, Hope quietly grabbed her in a side hug and laughed. "I think thou doth protest too much."

"What's that supposed to mean?" She crossed her arms.

"Not for me to say." Hope snickered and headed over to the group with a puzzled Anne trailing behind.

Hope was making introductions. "Sheriff, this is Beth Nelson. Dr. Nelson, the decease—is in the gazebo."

"Missus Nelson, I think it would be good if we went into the house. I'll need to ask everyone some questions." It wasn't framed as a request but an order.

Beth and Liz clung to each other as Taylor and Hope followed. Anne turned back when she didn't see Lil. The woman was facing toward the gazebo. Was Anne mistaken or had she heard a whispered 'I'm sorry' from Lil?

86

When Kandi got out of her truck and spied the paramedics, she dropped the two bags she was carrying.

"Not again," Kandi cried out.

Anne ran up to her and caught a shivering Kandi in her arms. It had been Kandi who had found poor Mr. Rogers not far from that same spot. Anne reached down and handed one bag to Kandi while she picked up the other one. "Nothing like last time. I assure you. Now, let's go on into the house."

Kandi nodded, her chin quivering and on the edge of tears. She choked out "Okay."

"Come on, sweetie. I think the ladies inside could use a nice cup of sweet hot tea." Was it just because of the incident or did it feel like the temperature had dropped quite a bit while they'd been standing outside? She looked up in the sky, and it still looked clear but in the distance were some dark clouds.

Oh no, not snow. Anne sighed. *Could things get any worse this weekend?* She needed to check out the weather report soon.

They walked toward the back of the house when a tall, lanky man with sandy blond hair strode around the corner. Out of his usual paramedic uniform, he wore a chambray shirt under a Carhartt jacket and blue jeans. All of the women turned their head toward him. One thing about Sam Powers, he was definitely attractive. So why didn't Anne want to take the relationship further than a few dates? She realized that where other women had to have a man in their life to complete them, she was happy to have her freedom for the first time in a very long time. So maybe it was all timing. And, as they say, time would tell.

Kandi perked up seeing Sam and bounded over to him where he enveloped her in a hug. "Hey, Candy-cane, good to see you too."

He released her. She looked up into his face. "When did you get back?"

"Last night. That's why I wasn't on call yet. But when I heard the address on the scanner, I drove on over." He smiled over at Anne.

"Sam."

"Anne."

A loud male voice broke their intense conversation. "Hey, Sam, may I speak with you for a moment?"

"Sure, Carson. Coming." Sam walked toward the sheriff.

Anne and Kandi caught up with Taylor and Lil.

"My, oh my, if he ain't a nice, tall drink of water." Taylor mimicked fanning herself.

Lil nodded.

"Ladies, how about a nice cup of hot sweet tea?" Anne switched the shopping bag to her other hand.

"Sounds good to me," Lil responded. "I feel a bit cold out here."

Anne agreed. "Yep, that's Colorado weather for you. I'm thinking we could get some snow tonight."

"Got any popcorn? For some reason, I'm in the mood for some," Taylor said.

After all the ladies had gone inside, Anne struck up a fire in the living room fireplace where she encouraged everyone to gather. Hope and Kandi had gone to the kitchen to make hot tea for everyone. Taylor had gone to help make some popcorn. Anne was dismayed to see Marie excited to be in the midst of the crisis. Anne could imagine the stories Marie would be thrilled to share. Nothing she could do about it now.

As Sheriff Carson took down names and addresses, Hope and Kandi passed out the tea. Taylor brought in a large bowl of buttered popcorn and some small bowls. She was the only one to eat some. Beth sat in a chair and rocked back and forth. Liz stood by her, silent. Lil had gone and stood by the fire, warming herself with her back to the group.

Anne noticed movement and went to the window across the large hall. Snowflakes. She groaned, and Kandi came up beside her.

"Everything okay, Mom?"

"Yes, I'm just wondering if we'll have a shark tsunami next. It's like one bad thing keeps building on the others. I'm afraid our opening weekend is going to be our last. I doubt anyone will stay for the full weekend, so that means refunding their money."

"Well, like I always say, it is, *like,* what it always is."

Anne made a face. "Not sure what that means, but okay. Thanks for trying to cheer me up."

Kandi lowered her voice. "You don't think one of them"—she nodded back to the living room—"you know, *like,* helped him along to meet his Maker."

"I don't know." Anne took a sip of the tea. She normally didn't care for sugar in hot tea, but it made all the difference now. "He had heart issues, so he probably died of a heart attack."

"Hope is always talking about the emotions and the body. She told me the heart has to do with love as a good

89

emotion but also as the negative emotion of hate or anger, and boy, was he an angry old guy."

Anne chuckled. To Kandi, anyone in their forties or above was old.

"I think that it's actually the liver that's associated with anger and the heart is more related to abandonment and loss of love."

"Whatever, it is. He wasn't a nice guy. But if you think it might be murder, then you better get those little gray cells to work."

"Okay, got it, Miss Lemon."

"Miss who?" Kandi's ponytail bobbed as she spoke.

"You know—Poirot, Miss Lemon, Hastings…"

Kandi looked up at Anne. "Is that a TV show?"

Anne sighed. "Then where did you hear about 'little gray cells'?"

"I just heard it, *like,* somewhere. I think—"

"Forget it." She nodded toward the group. "Might want to check and see if any of them want more tea."

As if on cue, Liz called from the other room, "Kandi?"

"See, you always know things." She headed off to Liz.

Carson had finished taking statements when Liz asked, "When can we leave?"

Beth chimed in, "Yes, I'll need to start making arrangements."

It finally dawned on Anne what had been bothering her outside. Beth hadn't cried then, and she wasn't crying now. It could be shock like Hope had said, but some time had passed now. Was she so cold-blooded toward the passing of her husband or was it because she had a hand in his death? Anne needed to get Sheriff Carson away from the group and tell him about the note and how Beth had pocketed the broken vape pen.

"I'll need all of you to stay in town for the evening in case I have any further questions. Pending any other circumstances, you should be able to make arrangements to travel home tomorrow," Sheriff Carson announced.

Kandi came around the corner holding a tray of finger sandwiches. "Ladies, I've made up some sandwiches and also heated up some potato soup."

Taylor rose and followed Kandi into the dining room. Each of the ladies moved behind them in a procession of downcast faces.

Once Anne saw that they were all in the dining room, she said, "Sheriff, I need to talk to you about a couple of things."

"Hold on. I need to speak to the medical examiner first before she leaves."

Carson looked over Anne's shoulder, and Anne turned to see Marie standing behind her. "What can I do to help?"

"I think we're good, Marie," Anne replied. "I would so appreciate it if you could sit with the ladies. They could use a sympathetic ear."

Marie nodded heartily. "Yes, yes, of course."

"How about we go to my office where we won't be disturbed?" Anne motioned for Carson to follow her.

He pointed toward the back. "I just need a quick word, then I'll join you."

Anne watched as the sheriff spoke to the medical examiner, a woman in her fifties who wore her hair in a no-nonsense brush cut. As they talked, she opened the door to her vehicle and slid out the large box she carried inside.

Once he returned inside, Anne ushered him into the office where she took a seat on the chair in front of the desk.

"That was a great save. Sympathetic ear." Carson grinned down at Anne. Apparently, he knew of Marie's tendencies for gathering gossip.

"Thanks." She pointed to another chair adjacent to hers but he stayed standing.

"You can sit down, you know."

"I'll stand. Thanks." He crossed his arms.

She didn't like the idea of him looking down on her any more than he already was, so she stood up again. She pulled the paper from her pocket.

"I found this in the Nelsons' room when I was cleaning it last night." She held it up to Carson, but he stopped her from handing it to him.

"Hold on. Back in a second." She ran into the kitchen where she retrieved a plastic baggie and stuck the note inside. She then handed it to him.

"And you found this in the deceased's room?"

Anne shivered. "Yes, I'd gone in for the turndown, and it was crumpled up. I guess they'd missed the wastebasket." *Forget this standing up. I'm exhausted.* She sat down. "Plus, when we found Dr. Nelson—the deceased, I mean—wait, let me back up."

Carson took a deep breath. He must have decided that Anne's story was going to take some time as he moved the chair away from the desk and sat down. They were now facing each other and Anne was having a hard time concentrating. Maybe the man's death had been more of a shock than she had thought.

"Ms. Freemont . . . " He waved at her to continue.

"Look, I know that you're supposed to call me that . . . or I don't know, but my name's Anne, so why don't you just call me Anne."

"Or I could call you Nancy, if that's where your

story is headed."

Anne fumed. "Ha. Ha." When she'd become involved with another case he had referred to her derogatorily as Nancy Drew. She straightened her spine and said, "I do recall that I did help to solve that case, so you can make fun all you like."

He merely looked at her with a big smirk on his face. "Continue."

She plopped back into the chair. "We were all in the dining room making Marie's cordial. Let's see . . . we'd finished and Taylor, I think, said that Dr. Nelson was still in the gazebo. Beth said she'd go out and Liz said she'd go with her. Then Liz ran back and told us to call 911."

"Hold on." He held up a hand. "What were her exact words if you can recall them?"

Anne thought back. "Let's see . . . 'We need help. Edward's had a heart attack.' Yep. I'm pretty sure that's what she said."

"Interesting," He commented.

"What's interesting?"

He ignored her question. "Continue."

"We all ran outside. Beth had been bending over her husband. Then I think Beth backed up and we heard this big popping sound."

"A popping sound?"

"Yes, it was Dr. Nelson's vape pen."

He jotted something down in a notepad he'd pulled from his pocket. "Go on."

"Let's see. Um, Liz reached down and picked up Dr. Nelson's vape pen. The vial was broken where Beth had stepped on it."

"Where is this vape pen now?" Carson had been writing in his notepad and looked over at Anne.

"Beth, um, Mrs. Nelson, stuck it in her pocket."

"Okay, I'll go talk to her about it." He picked up his hat which he'd placed over his knee during their conversation. Running his hands through his hair, Anne noticed it being grayer than the last time she'd seen him. He stood and headed for the doorway. He turned to her, tipped his hat and said, "Good work, Nancy."

Chapter Eleven

Anne glanced out the window. The snow that had been light fluffy snowflakes was now coming down in full force. They'd probably get a few inches, if not more, by morning. She sighed. Nothing she could do about Mother Nature's whims, especially when it came to Colorado weather. She returned to find the ladies finishing their somber meal.

"Marie, would you like to stay for dinner with us?" Hope inquired. "We have plenty."

"That would be nice. I'm a bit tired though." She yawned. "Do you have a place I could take a nap?"

"Certainly," Hope responded. "It's not unusual to have a dip in energy after an adrenaline rush like we all experienced this morning."

Everyone else decided a nap sounded like a good idea and went up to their respective rooms.

After the ladies had left the room, Hope spoke to

Marie, "We have a small room that you can use. There's also a bathroom in the hallway if you want to freshen up before dinner." Hope headed toward the front stairs.

"Oh, can we go up the stairs from the kitchen? I love those old back stairs."

"I suppose so." The pair headed to the kitchen where Hope opened the door. She switched on the light which barely illuminated the worn wooden stairs.

As Hope made her way up the stairs with Marie following her, the door at the top of the stairs opened. Liz came out onto the landing. "Oh, it's you all. I kept hearing footsteps and I couldn't figure out where it was coming from. At first, I almost thought it was from the attic, but I guess it was you guys." Liz moved back into the hall as Hope and Marie reached the landing.

"When did you hear the footsteps?" Hope inquired.

"I hear them the most at night. I figure since I'm next to this stairway, I hear more of the comings and goings."

Hope didn't dare say that staircase was only used for taking down linens or trash. No one used it at night. "Would you like another room? We have another double on the far end that's available."

"No, since we'll only be here tonight, I'd rather not switch rooms. I'll see you at dinner." She went in and closed her door behind her.

Hope walked down to the next door and opened it to a small, but quaint, room with a twin bed.

"This is a lovely little room." Marie looked around at the small space.

"We figure that this will make a great arrangement for families when we have our annual homesteading fair. As you can see there's a communicating door between rooms. Right now, it's locked on both sides, but it makes a nice suite for a family. The bed is a trundle so two kiddos can sleep on it."

"You all have thought of everything," Marie responded. "That bed looks comfy for a nap. I'm also looking forward to enjoying Kandi's dinner tonight. She's a great cook. Thanks for asking me to stay." She stifled a yawn which gave Hope her cue to leave.

"Okay, we'll see you later," Hope answered. Marie closed the door behind her and Hope heard the door being locked from the inside. She glanced at the back staircase door, now closed, and walked to the main staircase. Reaching the stairs, she turned back and went to the door where the back stairs were located. Hope pulled out a set of keys and locked the door. That should take care of that issue of the footsteps.

Marie had just dozed off when she heard low angry voices from the next room. She got up and tiptoed to the communicating door.

"What do you mean 'did I do anything?' What kind of question is that?"

"You know what I mean."

"I'm not even going to justify that with a response. Of all the gall."

"You hated him." If only she knew their voices better. Marie cupped her hand on the door.

"You weren't such a big fan yourself."

A loud knock sounded on a door in the hallway, causing Marie to jump. She stifled a scream.

Another voice. She couldn't hear what they were saying.

She swung open her door to the hallway. Taylor stood in the hall by the door. From Liz's room, Lil appeared, followed by Beth and then Liz. All of their faces were livid with emotion. In turn, they spotted her gawking at them. Only Taylor acknowledged her before retreating back inside her room. Beth passed her and slammed the door to her room. Liz went back in and shut hers. Lil stood in the hall, a mixture of emotion on her face.

Marie smiled and said, "See you at dinner." Lil nodded then went back to her room.

Back in her room, Marie sat on the edge of the bed and contemplated what she had overheard. Had it been two voices? Three? She couldn't make out enough of the commotion to distinguish between the voices. Maybe she could listen over dinner and try to figure it out.

Her excitement grew. Yet, it wasn't enough to stop exhaustion from claiming her. She slept.

After Marie woke up from her nap, she stepped out into the hall. Lights were on now and she could tell the sun had begun its descent. The quietness of her surroundings let her know that she was the only one on the floor. She listened to be sure. Only silence. She went over to the adjacent room and just as she reached out for the handle, she hesitated. No, much better to go and join the group and figure it out from there.

She moved toward the main stairs but decided to take the back stairs. It would be easier to come in and maybe overhear if she came from the kitchen. She opened the door to the landing. It seemed much cooler on the landing than when they come up earlier. The light had gone out on the landing, and she grappled for the light switch. Nothing. Well it wasn't a problem, she figured she could probably get down to the area lower where the light was still showing the steps. She sought to place her hand on the rail when a loud voice yelled, "Stop!" Cold hands gripped her arms and thrust her back into the hallway. A bright light forced her eyes closed.

She screamed.

Chapter Twelve

"Marie! Marie! Can you hear me?"

Anne and the others had all run up the stairs when they heard Marie's screams. As they quickly took the steps, Anne heard a loud slam. That must be what Hope and Kandi had heard. Stewart had to get over here now. They couldn't have Marie spreading the word that the house was haunted.

Anne bent down next to her. "Marie, you fell and hit your head."

"No, I did not!" She forced herself up. "I was going to go downstairs." She shivered and pointed toward the back stairs. "But, when I got in there, the light on the landing was out. I figured I could use the hand rail and make it to where the light was shining below. But then a cold, dead hand grabbed me. A bright light hit me in the face and said, 'Stop!'"

Liz said, "Let me go take a look." She didn't wait

and headed to the landing.

"Please be careful. Don't go down the stairs," Hope replied, and the group turned their attentions back to Marie.

Liz returned and shrugged her shoulders. "Sorry, I looked and couldn't see anything. I even used my headlamp." She pulled it from her pocket and handed it to Anne.

"Let's all go downstairs and wait for dinner in the living room." The women paired up and walked down to the living room. Anne moved back toward the stairs with the door yawning open, and slammed it shut.

Hope pulled her over. "Anne, I . . . I locked that door earlier."

"Let's talk about this later. We really need to get down there with the ladies now and change the conversation." The pair turned to catch up with the others.

Down in the sitting room, Kandi had prepared a nice selection of canapés, hors d'oeuvres, and other pre-dinner delights. She had done a quick-change act in the backroom office and was now dressed in a cute outfit of a green suede top with brown corduroys tucked into brown leather boots. She'd pulled her cherry-red hair back in a high ponytail. As Kandi placed the tray on the hunter's table and passed out plates, Anne surveyed the room.

Hope had pulled Marie to the side and they were deep in conversation. Anne prayed that Hope could stop Marie's imaginative mind and tongue. The last thing they needed was a group of women in a house they thought was haunted. The pair left the room and Anne felt some of the tension she been holding release as Marie laughed at something Hope said.

Two deaths. She didn't believe in ghosts. But what had happened? Was Marie just making a story up for attention? Anne shivered. *Get a grip, woman, you're making yourself crazy thinking about these things.*

She forced herself to take a deep, calming breath as she looked around the room.

Taylor had put on a long blue sweater covered by a pair of dark blue slacks. She wore her ubiquitous sensible flats. She had been one of the first to secure a plate and the day's events hadn't affected her appetite.

Was that a sign of someone who was guilty? No. The woman worked in close proximity to death on a daily basis. She was probably just used to it.

She turned her attention to Liz. The woman had made some effort. She had on a maroon dress with a multi-colored scarf. Her hair had been blown-dry and soft waves framed her face, which was glowing. She was also the only one wearing heels. She leaned back in her chair, her eyes turned toward the snow that had continued to fall outside.

Hmmm, she looks all decked out for a night on the town? Or even worse, a celebration?

Anne turned toward Beth. She didn't look like she had done much other than change out of her clothes from the morning. Her hair was tucked behind her ears and she wore a wrinkled navy-and-white top with a blue denim skirt. She accepted the plate from Kandi and nodded half-heartily as Kandi expressed her condolences. Smoothing her skirt, Beth set the plate down in her lap but didn't eat.

The grieving widow. At least she looks a bit more like it now.

Finally, Anne turned toward Lil who had pulled her white-gold hair back into a twist popular with Doris Day in the sixties. On Lil, it looked right. She wore pearl stud earrings and a simple silver and pearl necklace. She'd finished the outfit with black slacks and black flats.

Lil is the only one wearing black. But that could be simply that the others hadn't brought black clothing on the trip or thought to wear it tonight. The group was subdued, nibbling at their food.

Taylor spoke, breaking the awful silence, "Kandi, these are so yummy. Thank you for taking such good care of us at such a tragic time."

"Thanks." Kandi beamed. "And you're welcome. Dinner is just about ready, and we'll eat in about thirty minutes if that works for you all." She gathered up the trays and headed back to the kitchen just as Hope appeared in the doorway. Hope had gone home and changed into a long brown skirt and tan long-sleeved top. She'd added a locally woven belt low on her hips and a fun, funky multi-colored vest. She'd used a bit of spiking gel on her short hair and she looked great.

"Hello ladies." She walked over and looked out the window. "I listened to the weather report and it says we are going to get about four to six inches of snow, maybe more. That shouldn't impede you leaving tomorrow, once the roads are cleared. Please know that we will be providing you all with a complimentary guest pass for a stay at another date." She smiled at the group.

"Don't ya'll worry now. This was certainly not a typical weekend to be sure." Taylor rose and looked out the window, the snowflakes coming down fast and furious. "Whoa. That is some beautiful sight."

The other women came up and joined her at the window. Ooohs and ahhs were heard from the ladies. Marie had rejoined the group and was the only one to stay seated.

"I want to go out in it," Taylor quipped. "Come on, Beth. You come with me."

Beth shook her head no. With Taylor's calm coaxing, she relented. The women went to grab their coats from the hall tree.

"I left my gloves upstairs. I'll join you all in a minute." Liz headed toward the stairs as Kandi came out of the kitchen area and headed to the living room to gather the used plates and silverware.

"Where's everyone going?" Kandi asked Liz.

"Outside into the snow. Join us. I've just got to get my gloves from upstairs."

Kandi pointed toward the back. "We keep some spares in the back. Feel free to grab a pair so you don't have to go upstairs."

"Even better." Liz smiled.

Kandi grabbed her parka and rushed past Liz. Outside everyone stood on the cleared sidewalk in the front yard, their faces to the sky. Caught up in the wonder, they didn't see Beth start shaking. She bent over at the waist and clutched her arms to her chest. Anne rushed to her side.

"I'm, I'm . . . " the woman sobbed.

"No need to say anything. Here, maybe let me help you up to the porch." Anne took Beth's elbow and Liz, who had returned, took her other elbow. Liz tried to comfort the woman, but Beth shrugged away her attempt. Instead, she sat down on the porch swing and buried her face in her hands. As Beth's body shook with gut-wrenching anguish, Lil and Taylor knelt helplessly by her side, their eyes glistening with tears. The snow was coating everything, thick and quiet.

Something moved over by Anne's house. A figure in a hoodie and pants was moving toward the garages.

Kandi yelled, "Hey, you!" The teenager turned his head at the women standing on the porch.

Kandi waved at the boy. "You there! Stop!"

Instead, the boy turned away and sprinted across the cul-de-sac toward the back of Kandi's house.

Kandi pointed. "That's the kid that ran out in front of my truck the other day. I could have killed him!"

"Oh, that's the foster kid, Spencer Andrews." Marie had finally joined the group on the porch, no doubt afraid to miss out on any conversation. "All those kids just look for trouble. Mark my words, he's going to end up in jail. Little hoodlum." She sniffed. "It's too cold out here. I'm going back inside."

"Yes, yes, ladies. I think Marie has the right idea." Hope nudged the women back toward the house. Hope gestured with her eyes to the side. Anne turned to see a flash of brown headed toward the trees.

Oh no. We've got to get these women inside. The last thing we need them to see is a bear next to the house. Without a word, they herded the women into the house. After the women were back in the living room, Anne grabbed Hope's arm. "Was that a bear? It looked like a cub maybe."

"I'm not sure what it was. I don't think it was a bear, but it didn't look like a mountain lion." Hope took off her jacket and stamped the snow from her boots. "Listen, I'm going to have Autumn bring over some herbs to make a calming tea. Let me go call before the snow gets worse. The ladies can have it after dinner and it will help them to sleep better."

"That's a great idea. I'll want some of that tea as well, after Marie's stunt upstairs."

Hope nodded. "Marie is a bit of a snoop, but I've never known her to lie or make up stories for attention. Something is going on and we need to find out what it is. I'll call Stewart to come over now and look around again. There must be something we're missing."

"Okay. Plus, we can't have her attitude affecting the guests. She really upsets me with that holier-than-thou attitude toward foster kids." Anne rubbed her hands together.

"Yes, I hate when people put everyone in one category too. But I don't blame Kandi. He did run out in front of the truck. She's right. He could have been seriously hurt or killed if she hadn't seen him in time to slam on her brakes. That's why I tried to talk with him about it."

"On another note, do you think I should spend the night over here with you?" Anne queried.

"It probably wouldn't hurt." Hope removed the scarf from around her neck. "One of us needs to sleep on the same floor with the guests and the other one down in our office bedroom."

"Sounds good. Right after dinner I'll go home and grab an overnight bag. Now we probably need to get the ladies settled at the dinner table. Do you want to check with Kandi and I'll round up the ladies?"

Anne gathered the ladies back into the dining room. Taylor and Lil went to take their seats while Beth stared at the head where Edward had sat.

"The table looks lovely," Lil remarked.

"Thank you," Anne replied. She'd used the gathered elderberry branches and dried flowers that Marie had brought with her. In between the branches and cluster of dark and lighter berries, she'd added short white tapered candles set in aspen containers. In the middle of the table, in a place of honor sat Marie's elderberry cordial, glowing in the soft lighting.

"You all have a wonderful dinner," Anne said.

"You're not going to eat with us?" Beth spoke up.

Hope replied, "We normally sit in the kitchen during dinner."

"Oh, please have dinner with us," Taylor exclaimed.

"Yes, do, unless you really prefer to stick with your routines. We wouldn't want to change anything," Liz remarked.

Anne nodded. Better to stick close to this group. Hope took one end of the table and Anne the other end.

Marie made a big show of picking up the cordial. She then made her way around the table stopping at her place. As she went to pour the cordial, Liz reached toward the branches and in the process knocked over Marie's glass. Cordial seeped into the placemat and across the table, landing on Marie's chair and the floor.

"Oh, I'm so sorry, Marie. How clumsy of me." Liz mopped up the cordial with her napkin. "Please trade seats with me."

Beth stood up and backed away from the table. "I'm sure her place can be cleaned up. Why can't you just let things go? Always trying to fix things. Helping out. Why can't you leave things alone?"

Anne was shocked at Beth's tone. Hope moved quickly to Beth's side. "It's not a problem." She helped Beth sit back down and they put some napkins under the area where Marie was sitting.

Marie moved over to Liz's seat while Hope moved the wet chair away and pulled up a chair from the corner. Liz thanked Hope and sat down.

Marie poured her glass and held it up to the light. As she spoke, the ladies were passing around the platters. Kandi had made roast beef, mashed potatoes, and a roasted vegetable medley. Marie took a healthy sip of the cordial. Her face took on a strange look.

"This tastes—" Her eyes grew wide and she began shaking. Her hand dropped the goblet, shattering the glass on the table.

Those with raised glasses hastily set their goblets back down on the table and stood up.

Hope rushed over to Marie. The woman had slumped down in her chair. Her face paled.

Hearing the commotion, Kandi rushed into the room followed by an ashen-faced Autumn.

"Kandi, call an ambulance!" Hope commanded.

With Anne's help, they laid Marie down on the floor. Taylor had come over and took up the woman's hand, using her watch to take Marie's pulse while Lil elevated her feet up on a chair. "Her pulse is very irregular."

Beth and Liz stood clutching each other. Hope's eyes told Anne what she feared.

Lil spoke quietly, "She's been poisoned."

Liz screamed, "Someone tried to kill me!"

Chapter Thirteen

The women had all been taken out of the dining room and were back up in their rooms. Hope had covered Marie's body with a sheet and they locked the door into the dining room.

Kandi met Hope and Anne in the hallway, motioning for them to join her in the kitchen. "I just heard on the radio that a blizzard is about to hit us." She pointed toward the kitchen. "Also, Stewart's here."

Hope nodded. "I'll call and get Sorcha to come over and stay with mom and Missy. Let me go talk to Stewart."

Sam and the other paramedics had arrived. They were waiting on the medical examiner to take Marie's body away. Sheriff Carson stood at the dining room door and watched as the crime scene investigators worked the scene inside. He motioned to Anne and she took him back to the office. She closed the door behind her.

"Now it looks like we could have two murders on our hands."

"Two?" He looked down at her.

"Don't you see? Someone must have killed Dr. Nelson and then killed Marie, who you know is a snoop. Maybe Marie found out something she shouldn't know, although she sat at a different seat, so it must have been meant to kill Liz. But maybe it had something to do with the ghost Marie saw."

"Whoa, whoa, whoa." Carson held up his hands and motioned for her to take a seat. "Ghosts? When did we start dealing with ghosts?" He shook his head and Anne bristled. She knew he already thought she was a bit of a kook.

He went on, disregarding her look of frustration. "Let's deal with the current death situation first. Right now, we have one death that looks to be a heart attack, but we won't know until the autopsy is complete. Marie's death is definitely more suspicious, but again, we don't have all the facts. Let's start with those."

A knock on the door sounded and Carson commanded, "Enter." He was obviously used to being in charge no matter where he was.

"Hey, Sheriff," the deputy spoke. "They'll be here for a few more hours. There's a call on the radio from dispatch. They've shut down I-70 due to the blizzard and there's been a ten-car pileup on the road leading out of town. We need to go work the scene, sir."

Carson nodded. "Permission granted, Ruiz. I'll take statements and meet you in forty."

"Yes, sir." The deputy tipped his hat to Anne and left the room, closing the door behind him.

Carson pulled his notepad out and motioned for her to start. Anne told him about the meal and how Liz had accidently spilled Marie's drink. They then switched seats. They had been passing around the food when Marie took a sip and then fell back into her chair. Lil had been the one to say that she'd been poisoned.

"Okay, so Lil made the pronouncement that Marie had been poisoned. Correct?" He continued to write.

"Yes."

"How does she know that?"

"Oh, Lil's a big researcher. She must know what effects poisons have and how they show up."

She stopped. Lil knows about poisons. Anne heard her tell Edward she was sorry after he was dead. Did Lil kill him in revenge for choosing Beth?

She looked up to see Carson staring at her. "Anything else?"

"Then Liz screamed. She said someone had wanted to kill her instead of Marie."

Had the poison been meant for Liz? What reason would someone have to kill Marie?

Anne continued, "Plus, we have the note. All this time I've thought it was meant for Dr. Nelson or Beth. But what if Beth had written it and decided against giving it to someone? Maybe to Lil." She clasped her hands together. "Or what if Lil had been the one who wrote the note to the doctor?"

Carson stopped writing. "Let's hold off on all the suppositions for now. Tell me about this 'ghost' Marie claims . . . claimed she saw."

"That's another weird thing." Anne responded. "We all—me, Hope, and Kandi—have all been hearing noises."

"Like what kind of noises?"

"They vary. Sometimes it sounds like footsteps. Especially on the back staircase but also in the hall. Then a loud banging every once in a while." Anne scooted forward. "Earlier, Marie was going to use the back steps and she said a cold hand reached out and stopped her from going down the steps. Then a bright light hit her eyes so all she could see was a figure all in white."

"Hmmm." Carson stopped writing. "Have you gone up in the attic to check it out?"

Anne pushed her hair behind one ear. "Yes. We had Stewart come over and take a quick look-see, but he didn't find anything. The shutters are all secure too."

"I think we should go up and take a look at the back staircase." He rose from his seat and Anne followed him. He stepped to the door and waved her through first and stepped aside to let her pass.

"Do you want to go up the front stairs or the back stairs?" Anne inquired.

"I think the front stairs." They walked together and went up the stairs to the landing. In the hall, the doors were shut to the rooms. "Whose room is whose?"

Anne pointed out the rooms. On their right was where Edward and Beth's room was located. Across from them a narrow door revealed a small room that had been converted into a storage closet. On the left from the landing was the small room where Marie had napped, and next door was Liz's room.

Directly across the hall from Liz was Lil's room and next door was Taylor's room. Anne noted that they shared a connecting bath.

He bent down and spoke quietly in her ear, "Now where was the note found?"

Good thing I'm a modern, capable woman or this is where I'd be swooning over his masculine charm. She giggled at the thought.

He looked at her, and she could tell he decided

112

against saying anything.

She pointed to the Nelsons' room. He nodded. "Okay, let's check out Marie's room." Inside, the bed linens were crumpled from where she'd been napping, but nothing else looked out of place. Anne noticed a wadded-up tissue next to the communicating door. She went over to it and realized that you could easily listen in on the conversation in the next room. She moved closer and overheard Liz talking about flights. Anne couldn't blame her for wanting to get away from whatever was going on here, but she had begun to have her doubts of anyone leaving with the blizzard coming, and now Marie's death. No one was going to Denver tomorrow.

They left the room and Carson followed Anne toward the back stair. "This is some beautiful old paneling on these walls." He ran his hand over the highly-polished mahogany. "Expensive for that time, too."

"Yes, at first, we thought it was too dark, but we wanted to keep the integrity of the old house, so we left it as is. This house is the biggest on our block. I think it must have stood alone for a long time before the others were built up around it." She turned back to face the hall and a strange sensation came over her of being watched. She looked to see if Carson felt it too, but he seemed focused on the back staircase. She opened the door.

He pulled a flashlight from his duty belt and shone the light inside. The landing was dark. Anne thought Stewart said he'd fixed that light. As Carson shone the light upward, he remarked, "Well, what have we here?"

Anne sidled up next to him on the small landing as he directed the flashlight upward. The light bulb had been removed. "What? Who would have done that?" He shone his light down the stairs. The stairs hadn't been changed much over the decades since the home had been built. Wooden steps led down to the kitchen with a functional round metal handrail along the side. A large bulb attached at either end was the only form of any decoration. Carson shone the light back onto the landing. "Where does this door lead—the attic?"

Anne nodded her head. "Yes." Carson opened the door and shone his light up the stairs. He spotted the switch and flipped on the light, which illuminated the stairs. He headed up the stairs with Anne trailing behind. The door slammed behind her and she grabbed Carson's arm. "Don't worry, Nancy, I got you covered. I won't let any ghost get you."

"I don't appreciate your sarcasm."

"My apologies, ma'am."

For some reason, that made Anne even more angry. Still, she stuck as close as possible to him.

They reached the attic, which had once been one larger area, now stacked with boxes. Along the side were three cramped rooms that were probably former workers' quarters. A separate room held a claw-foot tub. An unused wood burner sat at the corner of the larger room.

Anne thought it must have been miserable to have lived up here in the winter or the summer.

They moved over toward the stacks of boxes which sat under a lower set of eaves toward the back. Dust covered every surface and the area was dark. Carson shone his flashlight around and then moved back and did a cursory search of the smaller rooms. Back out in the main room, he pushed a couple of boxes to the side sending up a cloud of dust.

"Looks like everything is fine here. Possibly an animal got in up here and is making its home in the rafters. And that could be what people are hearing. I'd get Stewart to do some checking for that."

He turned and walked toward the stairs back down to the second floor. Back on the main stairway, Anne told Carson about Hope locking the door.

"Interesting."

Interesting. Is that all he can say?

As Anne followed she thought she heard a stifled sneeze. She swung around toward the empty hallway. "Did you hear that?"

"Hear what?"

She shook her head and quickly caught up with Carson who stood in front of Lil's door. One by one, he knocked on the doors letting the ladies know that he would be asking them to come down to the living room. As they left, Anne motioned to Carson. "Let me show you where I found the note."

"Let's look later. I can't go search their rooms without probable cause."

"A woman being murdered is probable cause enough, isn't it?" Anne stuck her hands on her hips.

Carson headed for the main stairs then turned and marched back to the servant staircase. "What did you say that voice told Marie?"

"Stop," Anne replied.

"And she was getting ready to go down the stairs, correct?"

"Yes."

He went on the landing and shone his light on the stairs. "A-ha."

"What is it?" Anne looked to where he'd bent down and was shining his light on the wall.

"Look here."

She crouched over his shoulder and squinted to

where he pointed.

A nail jutted out of the wall. A bit of string was tied around it with a frayed end, as if someone had hurriedly hacked it off. The opposite side showed a hole where a nail had also been. "If Marie or anyone else would have stepped onto the next step, they would have fallen down the stairs. With the light out, no one would have noticed the string across the step." He stood back up.

"I want you to lock that staircase to the back area. Don't let anyone, and I mean anyone, go in there. Then take me to the nearest phone."

While Carson talked to the judge to gain a search warrant, Anne went back into the kitchen where Kandi, Hope, and Stewart had gathered. Autumn had brought the items that Hope had requested and was waiting with the others.

"Kandi, could you take Mouser over to your house for the evening?" She turned to face Stewart. "Any luck on our noise problem? Carson said it might be some kind of animal maybe coming in and settling in the eaves."

Stewart replied, "I haven't been able to find anything. I looked at all the shutters outside. They all look secure, but I can't get up to them with a ladder or look at them until after this blizzard has passed. But if you want I can go back up to the attic and take a look around. I also thought I'd check out the basement. Maybe it's some air in the pipes that are causing the booming sound."

"Good idea. I never thought of that and it makes sense. I think it can wait, though. For now, it would be good for you all to head over to Kandi's," Anne replied. The group got up and Anne gave Kandi a hug. "I'll see you tomorrow. Now get on home before it turns into total whiteout conditions. She turned to Stewart. "You'll watch over my girl, right?"

"You know I will." An understanding passed between Stewart and Anne. If only Kandi could see how much that Stewart would do anything for her. He wore his love for her in flashing neon.

After the trio left, Carson appeared from out of the office. "Okay, the judge is granting a warrant. It'll be a while for it to come, through. Do you have a fax machine?"

"No. But he can send it to the hotel information email. If that works. Then I can print it out for you."

Carson rubbed his chin where a bit of stubble had appeared. "Hmmm. Not sure if that's okay with protocol but I'll call back and ask." As Anne turned to leave, he grabbed her arm, "Be very careful and tell Hope to be the same. Don't go anywhere in the house by yourself."

"You're scaring me."

He dropped her arm. "Good. We have a person that we know killed at least one person and may have killed another. I don't want a third on my watch."

"What should we do now? This storm is really picking up," Anne asked.

"I'm going to interview each of the women separately to see if any of them reveal any errors or slip and tell us some information. Let's get them all down into the living area so they can't compare stories."

Anne rubbed her hands. "I should sit in with you."

"I don't think so. You're not an officer of the law." Carson shook his head.

"You're not interrogating them, are you? I figure that you're just asking them some background questions. If they are with you alone, they could easily say anything. They could accuse you of harassment, or something even worse. In this day and age people will do anything." She

117

folded her arms across her chest. "Admit it. You need me."

Carson sighed. "Good point. However, this is only an interview. I want to see how they respond to some general questioning to get a baseline."

"That's all fine and dandy but you're pretty scary looking in that uniform. I doubt you're going to get much out of them. Why don't you let me just ask some general stuff—how they met, the trip here, you know, stuff like that. Then if there's anything in particular you want to ask, you can throw it in."

Anne could see Carson thinking. "Okay." He rubbed his chin again. "Let's try it out with one person first and see how it works. Who do you recommend?"

"I think Taylor. She seems the most forthcoming and could probably give us more insight into the friendships compared to the others, who seem a bit more tight-lipped."

"All right. Let me gear down before we start."

"Gear down?"

"I'm going to take off my duty belt. Do you have a safe?"

"Sorry, no," Anne replied. "It's on our list but we haven't bought one yet. But I can lock this door."

"Okay, go and tell Hope our plan. Then bring Taylor back. We'll question her here in the office."

Chapter Fourteen

Taylor walked into the office where Carson had pulled up the stool and the chair next to the desk. Anne noticed Carson had removed his uniform shirt and now wore a black long-sleeved T-shirt with the sheriff's logo on the chest.

"Ms. Taylor," Carson began, "we'd like to ask you some basic questions about the other ladies if you don't mind. Is that okay with you?"

"Sure." Taylor sat down in the chair opposite Anne, who pulled out a pad to make some notes. With the woman's focus on Anne, it gave a more casual approach to the conversation and Carson had given his consent.

"I'm just trying to get a handle on the premise of the relationships within the group. Could you expound on it?"

Taylor turned to Anne who said, "He wants to know how you all became friends, and all decided to come here." She winked at Taylor.

"Oh, gotcha." Taylor straightened and then said, "Um, where do you want me to begin?"

Anne said, "I've already told him you all met in college. So maybe from that point."

"We were such good friends. Like sisters." Taylor sighed. "Then old Nelson came into the picture. It changed everything."

"Go on." Anne encouraged.

Carson glared at her. She'd forgotten his admonition to not speak into the silence. She grimaced.

"Edward Nelson is . . . was, a charmer. I'll give him that. He could have had any woman in that college on his arm. And he usually did. He was known as a big-time player, but it didn't stop more women from trying to tame him. But it was no use. He had his heart set on one woman and no one could keep him from winning his prize."

"You mean Beth?" Anne asked.

Carson glared at her.

"Oh, no. Beth definitely had her sights on him, but he had eyes for one woman only."

"Lil," Both women said in unison.

Taylor glanced at Anne. "Yes, he fell head over heels for her. And Lil had fallen hard for him too."

"Ahhh, now it's becoming clear," Anne interjected. "So, after he'd won her over, he lost the thrill of the chase and was done with her."

Taylor laughed. "Oh, you've got it all wrong. He loved Lil. Still did, judging by his face when he saw her again. Lil was focused on becoming a doctor and she knew that a relationship would be a distraction. She tried to get him to wait on taking their relationship any further until after they'd graduated. But he wouldn't have it. He got angry. He went off with other women. He made Lil's life a living hell. He and his friends were always pranking her and calling her the Snow Queen. One of the pranks went wrong and Lil even got pretty badly injured."

Anne thought back to the large scar on Lil's arm.

"That was it. Lil applied to other universities. She ended up at Oxford College of Medicine. When Lil left, Liz became my roommate, so I still saw Beth and Edward. Of course, with Lil out of the picture, Beth really went to work on him. She knew he was weak. She made herself over to look as much like Lil as possible. Whatever she did worked. Beth got pregnant—most likely on purpose—and he married her. But that never stopped his wandering eye. Why she's put up with his affairs all these years I'll never understand." Taylor took a deep breath. "So, you see, he didn't dump Lil. She dumped him."

Carson spoke, "Okay, so it seems interesting that all four of you decided to come together for a weekend after all these years. Can you provide some insight on that, Ms. Taylor?"

"Yes, that was strange. I'm guessing it was"— she tilted her head upwards—"yes, about six months ago. Out of the blue, Liz emailed. Said she'd been thinking about me and wondered how I was. We got to chatting and she asked about Lil, you know basic catching-up stuff. I asked about Beth and she said their son was off in college." Taylor paused. "Anyway, she said we should keep in touch and try to get together. I agreed, and we started emailing back and forth and soon we began calling each other. Finally, she said that we should get back together if our schedules worked. She and Beth were thinking about flying into Colorado and wanted to know if I'd join them. That it would be like old times."

Taylor looked down at her hands. Anne started to say something when she caught a slight shake of Carson's head to remain quiet. Seconds passed, though it seemed much longer. "You know, I figured enough years had gone by that Beth and Lil could be together. I mean Beth had Edward, and Lil had married Brad and they have two wonderful kids. Of course, Brad passed away a few years ago after a terrible accident." She looked up. "Some kid. Texting. Seriously injured Brad and the kid texting was killed instantly. I helped Lil with him until he passed." She choked back a sob. "Insurance came through and Lil doesn't have to work ever again. She's always loved research though, so I doubt she'll ever stop. I feel she only came on this trip because she felt she owed me that. How stupid could I be not to realize this was a bad idea? And now Edward dead and poor Marie." Anne grabbed some tissues from a nearby box and handed them to her.

"Ms. Taylor." Carson's deep voice cut through the silence. "Do you believe that Marie was the intended victim? Can you walk me through your time arriving here, up to now?"

Taylor blew her nose and Anne handed her another batch of tissues which Taylor wadded into her hand, pulling at it. "You mean, do I think Liz was the intended victim? Why? Lil wouldn't want to hurt her. I know Beth and Liz have a bit of a 'frenemy' type relationship, but they always have, ever since college. Liz has always been there for Beth, being supportive when Edward was being his usual jerk self. She'd tell me some of the things he did to Beth and Liz would say Beth should divorce him and be done with him. She would always tell me how she tolerated Edward because of Beth. They were like real sisters, they love each other, but they also get on each other's nerves."

She took in a deep breath. "No, I can't see anyone wanting to hurt Liz, or Marie for that matter. She seemed nice enough."

"What about Dr. Nelson?"

"Nelson?" Taylor turned to face Carson.

"Yes. Would any of the three want to kill Dr. Nelson?" Carson asked.

Taylor shook her head. "Well, I'm sure they thought about. But jokingly. You know, not for real. Plus, he had heart problems. The problems had grown worse over the last few months."

"How do you know that?" He motioned to Anne to make notes.

"Liz told me when we would chat. He's always had hypertrophic cardiomyopathy." Taylor shifted in her seat. "It's inherited. He found out more about when he got into medical school and that's partly why he went into cardiology."

"So, he took nitroglycerin tablets?" Anne looked up from her writing.

"Oh, no. Anything like that would have made the symptoms worse."

Carson responded, "That's good to know, Ms. Taylor. Now, you all came here, and Ms. Freemont has told me that there was bit of conflict when everyone first arrived. Can you take it from that point up until now?" He sat back on the stool.

"Yes. I was really angry with Liz. She never told me the doc was coming. I'd asked Lil to come, and she wasn't happy to see the pair either. I told her Beth might come and she was okay with that. Like I said, we were like sisters until old Nelson got involved." She tore off a shred of tissue. "Beth was furious. Even while we were upstairs, I could hear her and Liz arguing." She faced

Anne. "As you know, I'm across the hall from them and Beth has never been known for having a quiet voice. When she's upset, everyone knows it."

Anne shook her head, confirming that scene with Beth on the first day.

"Liz told me that Beth had invited him at the last minute, so she had no way to tell me. She apologized and said she'd understand if we left." Taylor wiped her nose with the wadded tissue. "I went and talked with Lil and she agreed to stay, since he wouldn't be around for most of the time. She said the past was the past. Ancient history. Whether that was true or not, I don't know."

"Please continue," Carson encouraged.

Anne scowled at Carson. If she had to be quiet, he needed to follow the rules too. He saw her face but ignored her.

"Everything was good until Beth saw the doc talking to Lil. The green-eyed monster has nothing on her. She was livid. But Liz calmed her down and then we started the cordial class. When I went to the kitchen sink to wash my hands, that's when I saw him."

"When did he go to the gazebo?"

"Not a clue. I was upstairs when I think he went out there."

"Do you know if anyone went out there with him?"

"Again, don't know. I was upstairs."

"Who was upstairs with you?'

"Lil was in her room changing out of the clothes from our earlier walk. I heard footsteps in the hall so either Beth or Liz were up there. I didn't look out into the hall as I was also changing."

Carson pulled out the sheet of paper with the words 'Now it's your turn to suffer' written on it. "Do you recognize this handwriting?"

"Whoa. No. But that's a nasty piece of work to be sure. Where did you find that?"

Carson signaled to Anne to not respond. "Ms. Taylor is there anything else that you think might be of any importance for us to know?"

Taylor hesitated and then shook her head. "No, I don't think so. Yes, the doc was a womanizing jerk, but I just can't imagine anyone actually killing him. I mean who would benefit from it?" Anne realized that this is what Carson was waiting for—someone to start thinking aloud. She held her breath, afraid to break any momentum from Taylor. "Beth definitely wanted out. Liz told me that. But she wouldn't leave because she'd get pennies. With her son grown, she'd have no child support and her lifestyle, friends, everything would suffer." She stopped.

Anne could see the conflict on Taylor's face.

Taylor shook her head. "No. No way. I'm won't believe it. Beth wanted him and fought to get him. No way she killed him."

Carson rose. "Okay, thank you Ms. Taylor. Again, this is just an interview. If we need to clarify anything, we'll let you know." He shook her hand. "We'll be out in a bit."

He closed the door behind her. Anne popped up. "That's some story. I think it's clear Beth did it. She stood to inherit millions and ditch the cheating scum."

Carson laughed. "Hey Nancy, you still have some learning to do to understand the way these interviews work. We need to get everyone's story and then the dissection begins."

She hated when he referred to her as Nancy Drew but at the same time she realized he appreciated her insights, so she let it pass.

"Okay, who next?" Anne asked.

"If I'm right, and I am, Taylor will be sharing a bit about the questions we've asked, so this will do one of two things. First, it will make the others more aware of the questions we'll be asking, and second, they will wonder what Taylor said. That's why I think we need to go with the widow next."

"Oh my gosh. I forgot. How could I be so stupid?" Anne rushed to the door.

"What?"

"We all had to label our cordial bottles. Everyone had to write down their names, the date, you know. We need to check the note against the bottles."

Carson followed Anne over to the cabinet where the bottles were stored.

Someone had removed all the labels.

Chapter Fifteen

"Nothing we can do about it now," Carson said. "Let's continue the questioning with the widow."

Beth Nelson sat down. She leaned back in the chair and crossed her arms across her chest. Carson pulled the stool over closer to the desk where Anne sat.

"Missus Nelson, again, I'm very sorry about your loss."

Beth gulped, and tears pricked at her eyes. She tightened her arms. Anne handed her tissues. At this rate, they'd need another box.

"We just want to ask some basic questions about your friends. Did any of them hold a grudge toward you, your husband, or Liz?"

Beth sucked in a breath. "What do you mean?"

Carson had been right. Taylor had been the right person to start the conversation.

"Let me rephrase that. You all met in school, but

you later went your separate ways. Was this due to anything specific, or just everyone going on different paths?"

"First, I don't know if I want to say anything without a lawyer present."

"Do you feel you need a lawyer?" Anne interjected and, if looks could kill, Carson would have knocked her to the ground with his stare.

Beth faced Anne. "I know how this works. Who do you think is the first person they always suspect? The spouse!"

Anne quickly shot a glance over to Carson who had moved a bit away from Beth's peripheral vision.

"Beth, this isn't about anything like that. We're just trying to see if any of you could think about anything that might help figure out what happened with Marie. Sometimes it's the little things that you don't think are important that are very important. That's why we're just asking about your friendship. It's got nothing to do with what's happened here."

Beth relaxed a bit. She turned to Carson. "Is that true?"

"Yes. This is a simple conversation. However, if you don't want to answer anything you don't have to respond. We're just conducting an interview with everyone to get your thoughts on the other ladies staying here."

"Yep. Just some background. Are you okay with that?"

Beth uncrossed her arms and folded her hands in her lap. She sat quietly as no one spoke. "I guess that's okay." She sighed. "But I can't see anyone doing anything—"

"Let's just stick with how you all met," Carson

interrupted.

Beth looked at him, then spoke to Anne, "In college we all hung out together. We had so much fun together. We really were like sisters." She paused. "Then Ed— Edward came into the picture."

"I bet he was very handsome as a young man," Anne replied, trying to draw Beth back into the past.

"Oh, he was. Is . . . was." She stopped.

Anne and Carson waited for her to compose herself and continue.

"Every girl on campus wanted him. Of course, all four of us would talk about him. Taylor didn't really want much to do with him. Liz was dating someone at the time, so she was also not in the game. Basically, it was Lil and me.

"There was a competition between you two for Dr. Nelson?"

"No. Not really. I did want to date him, but I wasn't one to go chasing after a man. Never have been." She crossed her legs, tucked her hair behind her ear and wiped her nose with a tissue.

That's a different impression than Taylor had given of Beth's infatuation with Edward.

Beth continued, "It was obvious Lil was head over heels in love with him. They dated for quite a while, but Ed later told me how she'd become too clingy, so he dumped her. She ended up going to college somewhere overseas and we would see each other occasionally over the years, but it pretty much tapered off."

Anne nudged her forward. "But you stayed in contact with Liz?"

"Yes. Liz has always been around. We've gone through a lot together."

"Liz never married?"

"She was in a bunch of relationships over the years, but she said she hadn't found 'the one.' She often joked she didn't want to end up with someone like Edward."

"No love lost there then?"

Beth laughed. "They were like fire and ice. Constantly bickering to the point that I had to ask them to stay away from one another. Then they'd be better for a while and it would start up again. Liz would get so angry with me about some of the things he would say to me. She tried to get me to think he was cheating on me." She uncrossed her legs.

"Now I know that he was a big-time ladies' man in college, but that all stopped when he married me. He always says I'm his rock."

Anne wished she could see Carson's expression. It sounded like Beth was going to deny Edward's womanizing ways to them. But it was interesting that she was still talking about him in the present tense. Was she still refusing to believe he was dead?

"Thank you, Missus Nelson. Now can you tell us about your coming here and all you can remember up until today."

Beth rocked her legs a bit back and forth. Anne quickly recognized the sign of stress.

"I got a call from Liz about a girls' getaway with Taylor in the Colorado mountains. We would come up here and do the workshop, then head on over and do some skiing before going to the hot springs. Jake, that's my son, had just gone back to college and I thought it sounded good, so I said yes. Taylor's always been fun, so I looked forward to seeing her again after all these years. I needed a break too."

"You said a girls' getaway. Why did Dr. Nelson come along?" Anne inquired.

"Um, well, I had said something to Ed and he was okay with me going. But then the next thing I knew, he wanted to come too."

Carson intoned, "Do you know why he invited himself?"

"He was going to go skiing while we had the workshop. I didn't want him to come but Liz said I should have him around to keep an eye on him. She was still on this kick that he was cheating on me." She smiled, but it didn't reach her eyes.

"Okay, so you got here and discovered that your two friends from college were also here."

"Yes, I laid into Liz on that one. I knew that Taylor was going to be here. But I don't like surprises. Especially with Lil being here. I wanted to leave right then and there, but Edward told me to stop acting so immature. That it had been twenty years ago." She sighed. "Of course, he was right. But I really want to leave now. I want to go home. How much longer will we have to stay here?"

They all glanced over to the window that bore a white covering of snow. The howling wind had continued unabated and the snow had been unrelenting as well. No one would be leaving until the blizzard stopped. Carson had already informed Anne that his deputies and the local police were all scattered around the area, sheltering in place from the storm.

"As soon as the roads are clear, you should be able to leave," Carson responded. "Now to the day of Dr. Nelson's death. Can you share with me what happened?"

"Taylor said Edward was still out in the gazebo. He had said he was going to head out after breakfast, so he'd been down there for quite some time. Liz walked with me to the gazebo."

She stopped. Her hands tightened.

"At first I thought he was sleeping but then, I could tell something was wrong. Liz took off running to call for help."

"Just as a reminder, you were with Dr. Nelson alone during that time?"

Beth stiffened. "Yes."

Anne jumped in. "We're just trying to get a sense of where everyone was during that time."

"Oh, okay." Beth eased forward on her chair, repositioning her body.

"Continue." Carson motioned.

"I bent down and touched his hand. I couldn't believe—he . . . that's when I realized that he was really gone. I just stood there. I knew Edward had heart issues, but you can never really prepare—"

"Again, I'm so sorry, Beth." Anne reached across the desk toward her. "I know this is difficult for you."

Beth swallowed and pursed her lips. Tears spilled from her eyes.

Anne shot a look at Carson who nodded for her to continue.

"I know it had to have been a shock. I think that's when we all arrived, is that right?"

"Liz came back, and she pushed me—"

"She pushed you?" Anne asked.

"Not like a push. You know, kind of like a grab to move you. I think she was trying to give me a hug, but I didn't want that. I didn't want anyone to touch me."

Carson spoke, "Okay, what happened then?"

"I don't recall much around then. I think the ambulance came."

"What about the vape pen?"

"What?" Beth turned to Anne.

"The vape pen."

"Oh, yes. I've been trying to get Ed to quit smoking, so he'd switched over to this vape pen thing."

"I believe you stepped on it. I heard the pop when we got down to the gazebo," Anne noted.

"Yes, I stepped back, and it must have been on the ground. I broke it when I stepped on it." She looked puzzled. "Why? What does that matter?"

Anne continued the story. "Then Liz picked it up and handed it to you."

"That's right. I just stuck it in my pocket." She turned to Carson. "One of your deputies has it now, I believe."

He nodded.

Anne wondered if they were doing any testing on the vape pen. Certainly, anyone could have put another ingredient into the cylinder. Even a higher dose of nicotine could affect someone with a heart condition. That didn't rule out Beth or Liz who had easy access to the device. As for Lil, who was telling the truth on who dumped who—Taylor or Beth? Lil could have been waiting for revenge all this time and with her pharmaceutical background, it would be easy to incorporate a deadly cocktail into a vape pen's cylinder. It also didn't preclude Taylor who was rooming across from the Nelsons and could have easily switched out cylinders. But what would be her motive?

Anne realized Carson was speaking. "Can you tell me a little about the time leading up to Marie's death?"

"That was horrible." Beth rubbed her hands together. "After Edward had his heart attack, we all went up to our rooms. I told Liz I wanted to leave as soon as possible. She'd booked our flights. I asked her to see about moving our flights up. I haven't told Jake yet. I want to tell him in person about his father."

Anne nodded.

Beth continued, "I wanted to stay in my room for the night, but Liz wouldn't give up. She said I shouldn't be alone, that I needed to eat something. I finally just gave in, so she'd quit pestering me. Later, we went downstairs, and Liz sat down next to me. Marie was talking about the cordial and then . . . I don't know, something happened, and Liz knocked over Marie's drink. She told Marie to sit in her place and next thing I know the woman was convulsing and—" She grimaced.

"That's okay. Thank you, Missus Nelson."

Anne jumped in. "Beth, I know this is putting you on the spot, but do you think that drink was meant for Liz?"

"I've been thinking about that. I think it was meant for me. and the sides got switched. That's why I want to leave. Someone wants me dead!"

Anne hadn't thought of that. But Liz had been sitting in the middle and Beth and Liz always sat together. Could the poison have been meant for Beth? When could Lil or Taylor have put the poison in the cordial? Certainly, Taylor had gone to the kitchen multiple times to visit with Kandi. Lil also went through the kitchen when she took a walk earlier in the day. Lil could have plotted revenge against Beth. But what was Taylor's motive? It didn't sound like Taylor held any ill feelings toward Beth. Was there something neither of them were sharing?

Beth was still talking, "Of course, as soon as Marie collapsed, Hope told everyone to not drink any of the cordial."

A shiver passed over Anne as she realized that any of them could have been killed if the cordial was poisoned. But how would the murderer have abstained? No, the poison had to be in the glass, not the actual cordial.

Carson reached over and retrieved the crumpled note in the sealed bag. "Missus Nelson, can you take a look at this for me?"

"Oh, that's horrible. Where did you find that?"

"This note isn't familiar?"

"No, I've never seen it before."

"Thank you. I think that's all for now. If you think of anything, no matter how insignificant, please let me know."

She nodded her head and left the room.

Chapter Sixteen

After Beth returned to the living area, Carson decided they should take a break before questioning Lil and Liz.

"We need to search their rooms," Anne insisted. "Maybe there's another note. Someone could have written a different one and not given it to Beth or Dr. Nelson. Or if Beth wrote it, then there could be a similar note in one of the other rooms."

"No," Carson said. "I have to wait for the search warrant."

Anne huffed. They were wasting time. She walked with Carson into the living area and told everyone that they could take a short bathroom break and then a late supper would be served in the kitchen. Kandi had left a pot of stew on the stove and there were two loaves of crusty French bread on the counter. Inside the refrigerator was a lemon walnut salad and two pies—a rich dark chocolate and a coconut cream pie.

As everyone sat around the table, Anne excused herself to head to the bathroom off the office. As she passed down the hallway, she realized she could go up and search at least one of the rooms closest to the back stairs. She tried her best to quietly make her way up the back stairs. At the top of the stairs she unlocked the door and made her way into the hallway. Hope had come up earlier with the guests and had turned on every light available to remove the darkness and gloom that had settled over the house. The falling snow caused a hush over the landscape outside and silence had settled on the house.

Anne pulled her keys from her pocket and opened the door to her left. Inside the room was brightly lit with clothes piled into a suitcase. She bent over the luggage and peered inside.

A hand pulled at her arm. She yelped and twisted away only to be looking back at the stern face of Sheriff Carson. He pulled the door shut.

"I knew you'd go and do something foolish like this. I told you that we must do things by protocol. You could destroy any evidence or mess up the investigation by your snooping. Now come on before someone—"

They could hear someone coming down the hall.

"Great. You may have cost us a conviction."

The door opened.

Without hesitation, Anne threw her arms up around Carson's neck and bent him over into a passionate kiss.

Liz stood in the door. "Oh, sorry!" She grinned. "I see I've interrupted."

Carson cleared his throat while Anne responded, "My bad. I didn't want anyone to see us, so I pulled him in here from the hall. I got sidetracked and thought this was the vacant room. I'm so sorry. I hope you'll forgive us. And please, don't say anything to the ladies." She piled on the innocence, hoping it didn't come across phony.

Carson said nothing, but his face was flushed red.

Liz responded, "No worries. Beth wanted her sweater and I wanted to grab my shawl, too." She went over to the desk and as she picked up the scarf, she glanced at her computer. She smiled at them again. "Well, I'll leave you to it." She left the room.

Carson looked down at Anne, his face red. Anne couldn't tell if the color came from anger or some other emotion. "What the—?"

"Hey, I just saved your bacon. We weren't snooping. We were making out." She crossed over to the computer. "Did you notice that she glanced over at her computer?"

Before he could say stop, Anne turned on the screen to reveal an email account. It was a message from Dr. Nelson's phone to Liz. It said simply, "I think Beth suspects us."

Anne turned to Carson who seemed a little too close now. "I think we found the person we need to speak to next."

Chapter Seventeen

Downstairs Carson and Anne entered the kitchen where everyone's attention was focused on a weather broadcast. Anne fixed Carson a bowl of potato soup adding a heaping amount of cheese and bacon bits on top. She had a hard time avoiding the pointed looks from Liz who smirked at her from across the table. At one point, Hope leaned over and whispered, "What's the private joke?"

"I'll tell you later, but it's a doozy."

After everyone ate, Anne and Carson walked to the back room. He turned to her. "I know why you did what you did. We don't need to talk about it. Smart thinking."

He walked ahead of her into the room. Smart thinking? Had he not felt that shock of electricity that she'd felt? Maybe he was right. It was the excitement of being caught. That's what it was. Nothing more.

Liz joined them in the office and as she sat down,

she made a sign of a zipper across her lips. "Your secret is my secret."

"Um, thanks," Anne said. "As you can imagine, we're trying to keep our relationship on the down-low."

Anne wanted to jump right to the big question of how long Liz had been sleeping with Dr. Nelson, but Carson took charge.

"From what we've gathered thus far, you are the one who suggested the girls' getaway. Is this correct?"

"Yes." She turned her entire body toward him and smiled charmingly.

"Did you invite Taylor and Lil to join you and the Nelsons?"

"I invited Taylor. She must have thought it was a good idea to have Lil join us."

"What about Dr. Nelson?"

Liz smiled coyly, and in that moment, Anne realized that they'd been had. The woman had manipulated them to view the email. How could she let Carson know? Was Liz trying to point the blame to Beth?

"Beth wanted him to come. But he was the one to decide to come and go skiing while we had our workshop." She shrugged and feigned innocence.

I'll bet that's why he came. Anne tried to hide her frustration at not being able to ask about their affair.

"How would you say the Nelsons' marriage is?" Anne hoped that was safe ground.

"Interesting," Liz replied.

Carson spoke, "Can you share with us about when you arrived and up to this point?"

She sat back in the chair and crossed her legs.

"Certainly. I'll try to remember." She took a moment and patted her finger against her lip. "Let's see. We arrived just a bit before Taylor and Lil. That really set

Beth off when she saw Lil." She sighed. "To be honest, it doesn't take much to set her off." She sighed again. "But I'm used to it. We've been best friends since college."

"Beth wanted to leave?"

"Absolutely. She did not want to be here with 'that woman' for one minute." She sat back in the chair and steepled her fingers.

"And by 'that woman'?"

"Lil, of course. Sweet, innocent Lil." She stopped. "Of course, everyone loves her. She's one of those people you just want to hate because they're so nice." She smirked. "Not me, of course."

"So, everyone liked Lil?"

"Especially Edward. He had the hots for her big-time in college. Then he switched gears and went with Beth."

Anne asked, "We heard he was a big ladies' man. Did you ever date him?"

"Date him in college? Oh, no. Too many cats chasing after that mouse." She grinned.

The Cheshire Cat has nothing on that smile.

"Let's get back to the day of Dr. Nelson's death. Can you tell me what transpired that day?" asked Carson.

Liz turned to face him, again she steepled her fingers and tapped her lips. "Let's see. We got up that morning and went for the walk. Beth was furious when she told me she'd seen Lil talking with Edward. I think with Lil's husband having passed away, it made Beth concerned."

"Why? Hadn't Dr. Nelson stopped the relationship in college?" Anne inquired.

"From what I understand, it was a mutual understanding to go their separate ways."

Anne wondered what the true story was—he'd left

141

her, she'd left him, or it had been mutual?

"Beth wanted to leave right away after Lil first came but I talked her out of it. I believe Beth even went and talked with Lil that evening. Lil told Beth that there was nothing between her and Edward after all these years."

That made sense as to the significant switch in Beth's attitude the following morning. Anne jotted down a note on the paper about it.

"Go on," Carson responded.

"Let's see." Liz paused, and her eyes looked toward the ceiling. After gathering her thoughts, she said, "We had the workshop. Then Taylor said Eddie—Edward, was still out in the gazebo. Beth decided to go out and check on him, so I said I'd go with her."

"Any reason for that?" Anne inquired.

Liz stared at Anne. "No." She turned back to Carson and continued, "I needed some air and I figured I'd walk with Beth. We reached Edward. I knew something was wrong. I ran back up to the house to get help."

"Did Beth tell you to go get help?"

She thought for a minute. "Yes, I think she waved me away, saying, 'Go. Go!'"

"Those were her exact words—'Go'?"

"I believe so." She picked at some unseen lint on her sweater.

"After that, I ran back to be with Beth. I tried to hug her, but she pushed me away."

That was different than what they had heard from Beth, that Liz had pushed her.

"What about the vape pen?"

"The vape pen?" She turned toward Anne.

"Yes. If you could say where it was?"

"Oh, yes, I see. Beth stepped on Edward's vape pen.

She detested his smoking. She wouldn't let him do anything, really. He was always trying to appease her to no avail." She rested her hands on the chair arms. "I heard it break so I bent down and picked it up. She told me to give it to her and I did. You know the rest."

"Okay." Carson nodded. "Now what about the time after Dr. Nelson's death and leading up to the misfortune in the dining room?"

"That was a strange afternoon. Marie screamed a ghost had attacked her. To be honest, it creeped me out a bit as I'd been hearing footsteps, but when I'd go look no one was in the hall."

Anne spoke up. "Did you ever go look on the back staircase?"

"I opened the door, but I didn't go down the stairs. Just on the landing." She stopped for a moment, then continued. "Oh wait, I think I did start to go down the steps but then decided against going down that way."

"The door wasn't locked then?"

Liz looked at her. "I couldn't have gone in if the door didn't open."

Carson shifted his stance. "Did you see anything on the landing or stairs?"

"Like what?" Liz turned toward him.

"Anything," he replied.

"Can't say if I did."

"Okay," Anne answered. "Let's return to your argument with Beth."

Liz turned back toward Anne. "Beth and I got into a bit of a row because she wanted me to update our flights. How am I supposed to know how long we'd be stuck here? I don't know why she wants to leave so badly. I know she needs to tell Jake and make arrangements but she, well, to be honest she said some nasty things to me."

She looked down toward her lap and clenched her hands together. "She doesn't seem herself lately."

"Maybe because she found out you'd been sleeping with her husband?" *Crud.* Anne realized her gaffe as soon as it left her lips. Carson shot her a look of disgust. She'd be paying for it now.

Liz looked up and stared at Anne who couldn't determine what was revealed on Liz's face. She definitely knew what it wasn't—shame.

"Okay, you caught me." She chuckled and shrugged her shoulders as if it was a minor indiscretion. "Yes, we'd been having an affair. Jake is out of the house and Ed wanted to leave Beth. He was going to ask her for a divorce." Liz stopped. "You don't think . . . no, Beth wouldn't do that." She wrung her hands and looked down towards her lap.

The implied message was clear. Had Beth killed Edward before he could divorce her and leave her with nothing?

"We're not inferring anything. We're just conducting interviews."

Liz turned to Anne. "I know what you're thinking. 'What kind of a friend am I?' We didn't mean it to happen. It just did. I still love Beth and I'm sorry to have hurt her. I know she's going to hate me when it comes out. That's why I wanted this weekend. To remind myself that things could heal between us. I'm hoping she didn't have anything to do with Ed's death . . . or Marie's." She shook her head. "Maybe she meant to kill him and me too for what we'd done." She pushed her face into her hands.

Anne swallowed. She didn't like what Liz had done but she sounded sincere about caring for Beth and had certainly showed it while she was there.

Carson pulled the note from a binder and showed it to Liz. "Do you recognize this?"

"That's horrible." She shook her head.

"Have you seen this note before?"

"No. But I'd recognize that handwriting anywhere. It's Beth's."

Carson put the note back on the desk. "Okay, thanks.

"Are we finished here?" Liz tilted her head.

"Yes." He stood up and opened the door for her.

As she went through the door she turned and smiled up at him, "Just for the record, I deny killing anyone."

Chapter Seventeen

After Liz had left, Anne spun toward Carson. "Whoa. What do you think of her story? This keeps getting weirder and weirder. It has to be Beth."

He crossed his arms across his substantial chest. "What makes you say that?"

Anne rose and started counting with her fingers.

"First, motive. Money is a big motivator. If Edward was going to divorce her, and she had no money of her own, that's a super strong motive."

"I concur that she has motive."

Anne held up two fingers. "Means. She knew he was using a vape pen, so it would be easy to put something in it that would affect his heart."

"Agreed."

She turned and held up three fingers. "Opportunity. She could have a ready-made alibi by being inside with us and she could have easily put something into Liz's glass."

"The evidence seems to point to her, but we can't rule out anyone at this juncture," Carson responded. "However, those are all suppositions, not fact or proof of guilt. Remember that old saying, "Innocent—""

"—Until proven guilty." She sighed and leaned her hands on the desk. "I know, I know. We just have to find the proof."

"We," he pronounced strongly, "don't have to find anything. You are in here only to assist with hearing their statements. That is all. You cannot share what you have heard with anyone or engage in any activity that could hinder this case. If you do, I *will* arrest you." He stood up and lowered his chin so that his eyes stared directly into hers. "Do I make myself clear?"

"Crystal." Anne sighed.

"Are you sure that she's guilty? What about the others?" he asked.

"I guess we should look at them too."

He chuckled but said nothing.

"Yes, I know, you can't rule out anyone at this stage," she said.

"Even you."

"Even me? Seriously?"

"You have the history of being around dead people—"

"Ha ha." She crossed her arms. "You're not funny and you're not taking this seriously."

"Oh, I'm very serious when it comes to crime."

"Okay, let's think about the others." Anne ticked off the points on her fingers. "Liz certainly had the opportunity. But if Dr. Nelson was going to leave Beth then she wouldn't want him dead. So, no motive. Lil could have motive with him dumping her but after all these years, it just doesn't make sense."

"Agreed."

"I just can't see Taylor hurting a fly."

"Ahh, that's where your personal feelings can cause problems. You have to look at everything objectively." He reminded her.

"True. I guess she could have killed Edward to avenge Lil, but what about Marie?"

"Some good questions. Let's switch gears. What about the means?"

"That one's a little tricky. Taylor and Lil have the most knowledge when it comes to pharmaceutical meds that could have been used in his vape pen and in Marie's drink. I wish we could get the toxicology reports back to know what really killed them."

"This isn't television. They don't come back with results in fifteen-minute timeslots."

"True. Plus, Edward's death may be totally natural. He could have just had a heart attack on his own. If we consider that, then the poison could have been meant for Beth or Liz." Anne stretched. "So that would leave Taylor and Lil."

Carson said nothing as Anne continued.

"But what could be Taylor's motive?" She paced the room, then paused. "On the other hand, Lil may not have gotten over Edward and that's why she really came this weekend. Her husband's dead and she knows Edward isn't happy. Maybe Taylor even knew about his affair with Liz or his desire to divorce Beth. If that's the case, then the message could have been written by Beth to Lil, but she decided against giving it to Lil and threw it in the wastebasket."

Carson sighed, but didn't interrupt Anne's out loud train of thought.

"On the other hand, maybe Beth wrote the note to Liz knowing she was going to kill Edward and make Liz suffer before killing her too."

He held up his hand with a stop motion.

"Lots of good speculation there Nancy, but in my line of work there has to be something we crazy officers of the law like to call proof."

She huffed. "Fine."

"Let's go ahead and get Lil in here. After we get everyone's statements we can start to see if any of them correlate or contradict someone else's story."

"I'll get Lil. Be back in a minute." Anne went to collect Lil.

The women were all together, yet separate, in the living room. While Taylor had plopped down in the chair, Beth had tucked herself tightly against the back of the couch and held a pillow protectively in front of her. Liz sat gazing into the fire while Lil perched on the edge of her seat, a pale bird about to take flight. Her back was straight and during the time they'd been talking with the others she'd plaited her hair into a French braid. She now wore a ruby velvet top and black pants. Anne was again impressed how striking Lil was without seeming like it took her any effort. Anne subconsciously pushed her hair back behind her ears. The pair walked back to the office.

Chapter Eighteen

"Sheriff," Lil spoke, "I'm happy to assist with your questions. What would you like to know?" She folded her hands demurely in her lap. Her legs crossed at the ankles.

"Thank you, Dr. Ryan."

"Lil. Please."

He nodded his head, "If you could give us a bit of background on why you chose to come here and the happenings up to this point, it would be helpful. Let's start with who invited you."

"Taylor invited me. She said that Liz had been talking about us all getting together at some point. I'm not one to cast doubt on someone's motives, but to be honest, I think Liz manipulated Taylor into inviting me."

"How so?" Anne leaned forward.

"I don't mean to speak ill of her, but Liz has always had the ability to get what she wants and manages to make it seem like it's the person coming up with their own idea. I can remember some of the things that Taylor would do for Liz while they were roommates after I moved out. Liz was definitely the one behind those ideas."

"So, you think Liz told Taylor to invite you?" Anne asked.

"Oh no, she'd never do that." She smoothed down her slacks. "She would have gone on and on about the good old days to Taylor, when all four of us were together in college. Taylor, out of all of us, cherished those times. She missed being away from her family and as an only child, we became the sisters she'd always wanted. For better or worse." She smiled.

Anne couldn't help noticing how white Lil's teeth were. She ran her tongue over her teeth. *Maybe I should check into some whitening toothpaste. I wonder* . . . her mind drifted in the silence.

Anne shook her head. *Stay present.* She watched as Carson waited in silence for Lil to continue.

He is definitely the most patient man. I'd be asking all kinds of questions.

"Taylor told me about this weekend at the Brandywine Inn that Liz had found online. Taylor knows I'm very interested in the flora and fauna that are used to make pharmaceuticals. For example, digitalis for heart patients, or the simple aspirin which came from willow bark. Ethnobotanical studies focus on the parts of the plant, and the best time for harvesting, preparation, application, and duration. Of course, it also includes the indications and contraindications of the plant."

"Oh, no," Anne yelped. "You sound like Hope. I only want to know what to take and when."

Lil laughed. "Sorry, I didn't mean to slip into

'professor' mode. I tend to do that now more than ever."

"You teach as well as do research?" Anne queried. Carson nodded approval at this question.

"Yes. After my husband died, I had lots of time on my hands. I've always wanted to learn more about plants in conjunction with my expertise in pharmaceutical drugs. I went back to school and now I'm teaching a course that combines the two areas. It's been well received, and Taylor and Liz have both sat in on my classes." She winked. "They're both geeks like me when it comes to medicine."

Anne leaned forward across the desk. "Wait. I thought you hadn't seen Liz in years?"

"I haven't. My course is available online as well. Taylor was taking my class in person, and I guess she told Liz about it, so Liz signed up for the online course. I have teaching assistants who grade work, so I haven't really communicated with her directly."

"You mentioned digitalis earlier. Is that what Dr. Nelson was probably taking for his heart?"

Lil replied, "I would expect he would most likely be on digoxin."

"Could he be on both?" Anne scooted forward.

"No. That could cause some serious issues." Lil stopped. She faced Carson. "Is that what happened?"

Carson replied, "We aren't able to comment on his death."

"Oh, of course." Lil regained her regal pose. "He wouldn't take nitroglycerin though. He has a heart condition that contraindicates taking it."

"Can you tell me how you know that, Dr. Ryan?"

"Certainly, Sheriff. We dated when we were younger and during college we all did medical testing and took medical histories on each other. That's when he told us that he had a heart issue and that it was his reason for going into cardiology."

"Let's talk about Dr. Nelson for a moment."

Anne watched as Lil twisted slightly to face Carson. "What would you like to know?"

"Tell me about the time in college after Dr. Nelson joined the group. Also, how the other three ladies in your group handled it."

Lil took a deep breath. "Edward was definitely seen as a prize catch to many of the women. His family had money, he had a great future in medicine, and he was good-looking. All the girls on campus were after him." She shrugged her shoulders. "For some reason, he chose me."

I'm sure it had nothing to do with you being beautiful, smart, kind, and humble. Anne wanted to dislike this woman but couldn't.

Lil continued, "The thing is once you got Edward away from all his fawning followers, he was a great guy. He had a quick wit, he was caring, and he wanted to make a difference." She stared past them as if looking back into that earlier period. "I admit I fell for him too. He wanted to get serious. He wanted the full-on relationship; engagement, marriage, kids, the whole works. I loved him, but I'd worked too long and hard to throw away my dream of becoming a physician. I told him that we both needed to concentrate on our studies."

"Overnight, he turned from Doctor Jekyll and became Mister Hyde. I think it was the first time in his life someone had ever said 'no' to him. He had his friends start calling me names and they'd pull pranks on me, but those pranks sometimes ruined weeks of research—" Anne watched the woman rubbing her arm, which she knew bore an ugly scar.

Lil took a deep breath before continuing. "He sought to hurt." She stopped, and Anne could see that Lil was holding back on saying something. "Then he started dating Beth. I'd come back to our dorm and he would be there with Beth and Taylor. He'd fawn all over her and Beth's gloating drove me crazy. I loved Edward. I felt used that he could throw me away so carelessly and take up with Beth so soon after our breakup. I struggled to stay focused and realized that my grades were going to take a hit if I didn't get away from them. I applied to lots of other universities and was accepted to Oxford. Edward and Beth married, and after graduation I married my husband."

"You realized your dream of becoming a doctor too?"

"Yes. MD and PhD."

"That's really impressive," Anne said sincerely.

"Yes. When I make up my mind to do something, I rarely let anything hold me back from achieving my goal."

Did that include revenge and murder? Lil certainly had the knowledge and capability. Motive, check. Means, check. Opportunity, check. Anne stared at Lil. Could this sweet woman really be a deadly murderess?

Anne finally spoke when the silence grew too long, ignoring the admonition from Carson. "So, it sounds like Taylor and Liz managed to not date Dr. Nelson." Anne was proud of herself for not letting the cat out of the bag about Liz's affair with Edward.

"I can't speak to Liz, but that's not exactly true with Taylor." She gazed down at her lap. "I'm not sure . . ." a long pause ensued, " . . . if I should be saying this."

"Anything you say is held in strictest confidence. It could be important," Carson urged.

154

"After we broke up, Edward got drunk. I mean, horrible drunk. He came over and was pounding on our apartment door. Taylor let him in. He cried about me breaking his heart. He'd brought a bottle with him. Taylor comes from a teetotalling background. She'd never had a drop of whiskey, much less a glassful. She decided to add some to her soda. Before long they were both in a drunken state and they started making out. The problem was that she was so out of it that she wasn't able to tell him no."

She closed her eyes and took a deep breath. "I've always felt so guilty."

Anne was stunned. "It's not your fault what someone else does."

Lil put her face in her hands. "If only I hadn't gone to the library that night. I could have stopped it." She looked up. "I came home, and Taylor was sick in the bathroom. She was crying about what she'd done and how her mind kept saying no, but she couldn't get it out—couldn't stop it. The day after it happened, Edward acted like nothing had occurred. For him, it was just a one-night stand. But Taylor was—still is—what you would call a good girl. She's never touched alcohol since."

"Did Beth or Liz know what happened?"

"Liz did. Taylor was crying one night, and she worked it out of her. I think she may have told Beth but I'm not sure." Lil sighed deeply. "I don't see what this has to do with now, though."

Anne and Carson exchanged a look. Had Taylor waited all this time to take her revenge on Edward? But that didn't explain Marie's murder. Had Marie seen or heard something she shouldn't have? Or had the poison been intended for Liz instead of Marie? Liz said the note was in Beth's handwriting, but could she have been mistaken? Was it Taylor who actually wrote the note?

Lil straightened her back. "What else do you want to know?"

"We were informed that you and Edward had a conversation at the gazebo before he died. Can you tell me what that was about?" asked Carson.

"He wanted to start over. He said he was leaving Beth and we could have a fresh start. He was going to retire from his practice and we could travel like we'd talked about in college."

Anne's eyebrows shot up at that revelation.

"What did you say?" Carson asked.

"I told him that he needed to make his marriage with Beth work."

If Lil only knew that he was cheating on Beth with Liz.

"Did anyone overhear this?"

"I guess anyone could have heard it. But I didn't see anyone around."

Carson thanked Lil and she walked out of the room.

"Geez, what a Pandora's box. That guy was a real piece of work. What a jerk."

"Why don't you tell me how you really feel, Nancy."

"Anne." She huffed.

"Let's let this stew for a bit and then we'll go back over it."

The lights went out.

Chapter Nineteen

Anne gasped.

"Take my hand," Carson spoke into the darkness.

Anne reached for him. A shock went up her arm as she grasped his hand. The electricity might be out but there were still sparks in this room. Had he felt it too? "I have a flashlight in the kitchen."

"Okay, let's go get it."

After retrieving the flashlight, Anne told him about the batch of headlamps they had used for walking. She pulled out the box while he shone the light on the contents. They had bought ten. Anne remembered that Liz had one of them, but that should have left nine. One was still missing from the box.

She showed Carson the box. She took one and he took the box from her. With his light casting a beam in front of them, they made their way to the living room. Hope had started the fireplace earlier, and all the women were subdued as the wind howled around the corners of the house.

"Ladies, we will all be staying here in this room until the lights come back on. If you would like to gather some things from your rooms—pillows, blankets or other items, you can do that and then bring them back here. We have these headlamps you can use. We'll take turns going up to the rooms and you can go by yourself or either myself or Anne and Hope can accompany you."

"I can go myself. I'm not afraid of the dark." Liz grabbed one of the headlamps.

"Liz, please also bring your other headlamp with you when you come back." Anne held up the box.

"Will do." Liz left the room and headed upstairs.

Lil stood up from the sofa. "Anne, could you accompany me upstairs?"

"Hope too," said Carson.

"Yes." Hope got up and the three left the room.

"Wait for me!" Beth yelped.

The hall was empty when they made it up the steps. Hope and Anne stood in the hallway as Beth went into her room and Lil moved down the hall to her room.

Lil returned with a pillow, blanket, and her purse. "I wasn't really sure what to take. Do you think Liz has gone down? Should we wait for her?"

The trio went to Liz's door and knocked. No answer.

Anne put her ear to the door. She could hear water running. "I think she's in the bathroom."

Beth came out of her room to make sure they hadn't left. She then gave them the thumbs-up and went back into her room. Lil joined them, and they made their way over to the stairs. Anne and Hope followed her down the stairs.

Anne reached out and pulled Hope close. She whispered, "I'm not going to kid you Hope, I'm really scared. I have this strange feeling we're being watched. I don't believe in ghosts, but first Ralph dies, then Edward, and now Marie. It's really creeped me out."

Hope rubbed Anne's arm. "Some people are more in tune with energy. My mother is like that. It's not really a lot of mumbo jumbo stuff, she is just able to read people and energy very well." She sighed. "But I know what you mean. This weekend has been very odd, and I've also had some strange sensations."

Anne could see Taylor as she walked closer to the lit fireplace. She heard Taylor say, "This is freaking me out."

"I'm sure it's just a transformer down due to the storm." Carson stood in the doorway and nodded at Anne and Hope as they stood on the staircase.

Taylor's voice carried up the stairs. "No, I mean what's going on. Yes, you couldn't have picked a worse time for a blizzard and the lights to go out. But someone here is a killer. What's to stop them from picking us off one by one?" Her voice quivered.

"Me. That's who," Carson replied. "That's why we're all going to stay here in this room together."

Hope and Anne remained on the stairs between the upstairs landing and downstairs until Lil made it to the living room. Then they'd go back up to get Liz and Beth.

Carson turned to Taylor. "You want to go up and get anything since Hope and Anne are already up there?"

Taylor nodded and put the headlamp on her head, switching on the light.

As Lil passed her on the way, Taylor reached the stairs. Hope and Anne tilted their headlights to better illuminate the staircase.

A scream caused them to grip the banister. Beth,

with a look of horror, was at the top of the stairs. She was pointing down the hall toward the back staircase. "A ghost! I just saw a ghost!" She stumbled down the stairs as Carson bounded up the stairs two at a time.

"What is it? I heard someone screaming. Is someone hurt?" Carson shone the flashlight all along the hall. He went in to each room with the trembling women behind him. "Oh no."

"What?" said Anne and Hope in unison.

"I told you that no one should be with anyone else on their own. Taylor and Lil are all by themselves."

The group quickly descended the staircase. "Don't go so fast. Don't leave me!" Beth shouted.

She turned her head and at the end of the hall a ghostly figure was moving toward the back staircase.

Her scream stopped everyone in their tracks.

"There it is again!" She broke down, hysterically sobbing.

Carson rushed back up the stairs while Hope helped the distraught Beth down the stairs to the living room.

"I'm sure there's a reasonable explanation for all this. Let's get you to the living room." Hope sought to comfort the hysterical Beth, while a shaken Liz stood next to the fireplace. Taylor and Lil had gathered on the sofa.

Anne was glad to see Liz in the group but how had she made it downstairs without anyone seeing her?

After noting that all the women were accounted for in the living room, Anne mounted the steps. Carson headed toward the back staircase door. He turned to see Anne behind him.

"Quick! Go back down and lock the door into the back hall." He waved with his flashlight.

Anne stumbled and half-slid down the stairs. Racing

toward the kitchen, she tripped and fell before making it to the door of the servant's staircase. She reached up and locked the door. Now limping, she hobbled back to the front stairs and climbed them to find Carson fussing with the door. "It's locked."

"Well, they're trapped. I've locked the downstairs door so unless they break it down, they have no escape but up to the attic." Anne reached into her pocket. "Here are my house keys."

"Step back." He motioned for her to move behind him. Carson quickly unlocked the door and shone his flashlight inside. No one was on the landing. The door to the attic was closed. Shining his light down the staircase, it too was empty. He turned his flashlight toward the attic stairs. His light landed on a hook latch that Stewart had installed thinking that may have been the banging that others had heard.

He shook his head. "Nothing."

Anne broke down crying.

"Now, now." He gathered her into his arms. "It's okay to be scared."

His embrace was warm, and she felt more secure than she had for days. She swallowed a sob. "I'm not scared. I think I sprained my ankle."

"It might be okay to be scared."

"Why do you say that?" Anne looked up into Carson's face.

"Because of this." He held up a sheet that had two holes cut out for eyes.

"We're not the only ones in this house."

Chapter Twenty

With Carson on her side, Anne managed to step-hop back down to where the ladies were. Lil moved out of the chair and Taylor gathered sofa pillows to elevate Anne's foot.

Carson said, "I'm going to go get some ice for that ankle."

"Let me go with you, Sheriff. I'd like to grab some arnica cream as well as make some herbal tea for everyone." Hope quickly reached his side.

He nodded. Then turning to the women, he said, "No one leaves this room. Understood?"

They all nodded.

In the kitchen, Hope lowered her voice. "What do you think is going on?"

"I don't know, but I'm going to get to the bottom of it."

"But first—" He headed off to the back office.

When he returned, his face told Hope something was wrong. "What is it?"

"My gun. It's missing."

Hope sat down at the table. Even in the dark room, lit only by the bright snow outside, the fear showed on her face. "So, we have a killer in the house who is intent on killing us."

"Don't worry. Whoever took it isn't planning on killing all of us." He ran his hands through his hair. "We can't let on that the gun is missing. Not even to Anne. Got it?"

Hope nodded. She shook her hands out at her sides and let out a long breath.

They returned to the living room where Hope handed Taylor the arnica ointment. As Taylor applied the ointment, Lil cut up part of a sheet to use as an ace bandage for Anne's foot, which was already swollen and turning colors.

"Ladies, here's some herbal tea for you." Hope passed cups around. "I also grabbed some of Anne's granola bar stash." The ladies took the tea and unwrapped the bars. No one spoke. The wind howled. Normally, the fire would have made for a cozy evening campout, but everyone was on edge, their eyes constantly flitting toward the hallway.

Carson moved over to the door and sat down facing the hall toward the kitchen and the front staircase. He leaned back on the wide wooden door jamb, presenting a human barrier between the living room and the hallway.

Every sound seemed magnified. The women huddled close to each other. Hours went by. Before long, the adrenal rush now gone, coupled with the hypnotic effect of the fire, the women began nodding their heads.

One by one, the women fell asleep.

A sound woke Anne. She glanced over to Carson, his body tensing at the noise. He caught her eye and put his finger to his lips. He leaned over and touched Hope on the shoulder. She startled but sat upright. He pointed toward the kitchen. There was definitely a noise.

He got up and quietly edged over to the dining room. With hand signals, he motioned for them to shut the pocket doors to the living room. Anne and Hope both shook their heads. He scowled at them. Hope went over and grabbed two pieces of firewood. She went over to Carson and handed him one. Anne could see he was telling Hope to go back to the living room, but she was having none of it.

Giving up, he motioned for her to get behind him and the pair crept out of sight. Anne felt useless as she sat with her foot up on the pillow. The throbbing had subsided, so she took the chance to stand up. Pain shot up through her leg. She hobbled on her injured foot and crept over to the doorway. She could just see Carson and Hope's figures moving slowly down the hallway. Each held the log tightly gripped in their hands like a bat. Carson leaped and a figure all in black appeared out of the darkness, headed for Anne. She screamed, and the figure turned, bolting up the main staircase. Forgetting her ankle, Anne moved to the stairs. As she put pressure on her hurt ankle, she stumbled and fell. Carson came around the corner and raced up the stairs, followed by Hope.

A door slammed. Carson ran down to the back staircase and threw the door open. He aimed the headlamp up and down the stairs. No one. Nothing. The door to the attic yawned its black hole. He cautiously climbed the stairs to the attic. As he reached the top, he switched off the headlamp he'd retrieved from downstairs. After letting his eyes get accustomed to the dark, he tentatively opened the door.

No sound.

He bent down and threw the piece of wood into the cavernous space. No attack. No response. Nothing.

Hope was now right behind him, arm raised.

Carson strode into the room. "This is Sheriff Carson. I'm going to give you three seconds to come out and then I'm going to shoot. One. Two."

"Don't shoot! Don't shoot!" A young male voice squeaked. Carson pulled the flashlight from his pocket and pointed it toward where a lanky young man was exiting from the stack of boxes. He stood up with his hands in the air.

"Spencer?"

"Sheriff Carson. I can explain."

"Oh, I'm sure you've got an explanation all right." He motioned to the boy who turned and went back inside the box. Carson followed. "Well, well."

Inside the boxes, Spencer had cut out the interiors so that it was long enough to lie down in and sleep. Some food wrappers, soda cans, and a dog-eared copy of *The Martian* were in one corner.

"Nice, huh?" Spencer remarked proudly.

"Do you know that people from social services are scouring the countryside for you? Mrs. Laurence is beside herself."

"I'm sure she's beside herself. Thinking about the money she'll lose out on with me gone."

Carson motioned for Spencer to exit the secret hideaway. They stood in the attic while Hope trained the flashlight on the pair.

"Okay, so let's have it." Carson stuck his hand out.

"Have what?"

"The gun."

"Your gun?"

"The gun you found in Ms. Freemont's office."

"I don't go in there. Someone is, you know, usually in there. I just get some food and I did borrow this headlight." He held it up for their inspection.

"Borrow, huh?" Hope retorted.

Carson searched Spencer's face for a moment, while the boy squirmed under the Sheriff's intense gaze.

"I'm telling the truth. No way would I touch a gun. They're dangerous."

"Okay." Carson grew quiet. "How long have you been up here?"

"Well . . . you know . . . "

"Have you been here this entire weekend?" Hope questioned.

He shrugged his shoulders but said nothing.

"You've been in this attic the entire time?"

"Well . . . " He shrugged his shoulders again.

Carson stared down at Spencer. "Son, a well is a deep subject. And I think you may be holding out on me."

"No. I wouldn't." Spencer held his hands up. He stopped, and his mouth twisted as he fought with himself.

"Okay look, you're probably, you know, going to find out anyway but I'm not the only one here."

Chapter Twenty-One

Downstairs in the living room, the commotion woke up the sleeping women. Taylor held a piece of firewood as a weapon, while Lil watched the door anxiously. Liz stood behind a chair, her eyes intent on the doorway. Anne had returned to her seat, the throbbing pain from her ankle making any action improbable.

Seconds ticked by. Then minutes. Finally, they heard footsteps on the stairs. Hope appeared in the doorway.

"All's well ladies. Nothing to worry about. An animal in the attic." Hope looked at the dying embers in the fireplace. No one had seen to keep the fire stoked with all the uproar. The first rays of light peeked through the snow-covered windows.

Then the lights came on.

Everyone cheered. Taylor and Lil hugged one

another.

"Ladies, if you would like to go get changed into some other clothes, I'd be happy to go up with you." Hope motioned to the stairs. Everyone agreed and they all filed upstairs.

Once they had reached the landing, Hope said, "Please stay in your rooms and I'll be back in a minute. And as a precaution, please lock your doors." She waved to the women and then headed down the stairs.

Lil stood in the doorway to her room, glancing down the hallway toward Beth's room. Beth came out of her room as Hope emerged from the storage closet with her hands full of clean towels. Once everyone was situated, she headed back downstairs. Lil moved into the hallway to join the others, when Liz exited her room. She was wearing a heavy sweater and boots.

"You going somewhere, Liz? It will be a while before the roads are clear," Beth asked.

"I thought I might go out in the back for a bit. Being stuck in this house has made me yearn for some fresh air."

"That sounds like a great plan. I'd like to get outside for a bit too." Beth went back inside her room where she grabbed a sweater.

From outside, the sound of a snowblower started.

The group made their way downstairs until they were in the kitchen. Hope was cracking eggs in a bowl. "Anyone up for some coffee and a breakfast burrito? I think we can get that started without Kandi."

"Count me in. I'm hungrier than a chicken on a June bug," Taylor quipped.

"If you can fix the coffee, I'll start on cutting up the vegetables," Lil responded.

Anne hobbled in from the front room. "Thanks for

getting this going. Not sure when Kandi will make it over."

"At your service." Hope winked at her. "Why don't you grab a seat?"

After Hope helped Anne get situated, she sat down next to Lil. Taylor was passing plates around the table and Beth poured coffee. Liz continued to stand next to the back door.

The loud roar of the snowblower cut through the air. *Carson must be clearing the driveway.*

Anne gratefully accepted a pillow from Lil for her foot.

"Come on, Liz. I've got cabin fever too, but we can go out after we eat." Beth motioned to the woman who still stood by the backdoor.

Anne glanced around the kitchen. "Hey Hope, you seen my phone? I thought I'd left it next to me in the living room, but I may have dropped it in all the craziness last night. I thought maybe it was in here, but I don't see it."

"Nope, but I can look for it after we eat." Hope took some fresh orange juice and began pouring it into glasses. She handed one to Beth.

"Thanks." Beth took a long drink of the juice.

The sound of a truck could be heard coming down the drive. Liz hoisted her bag onto her shoulder and went out the door. The ladies joined her on the back porch. Kandi waved to them from the door of her four-wheel drive truck.

"Hey you guys! Was that, *like*, some storm or what last night?" Kandi stepped down onto the automatic truck step.

"That was some storm all right," Hope replied, shading her eyes from the bright snow that covered everything in a heavy layer of fondant.

Kandi took a step forward. "What's, *like*, the emergency?"

"What?" Anne had limped out to join the group. She took a hop forward toward the railing.

"I got a text that said to come in the truck. That you needed help. Is it your foot?"

"I didn't send you a text."

Liz stepped over toward Kandi. "I did it." She faced Anne. "I saw your phone lying on the table and I was concerned you might have broken your foot, so I texted her. I've seen enough broken bones to know when something's broken." She laughed but it came out flat.

"Stop right there," Carson's voice commanded. He moved quickly from the side of the house where he'd been listening to their conversation. He stood in front of the women.

But if Carson had been next to the house, who'd been using the snowblower?

Anne looked out to the figure who was had been using the snowblower to clear the driveway. He was wearing Carson's coat and hat. He took off the sunglasses. Anne recognized the young male as the boy named Spencer. He pointed to Liz. "That's her. That's who I saw."

Liz grabbed Kandi, who screamed out in terror. From her pocket, Liz pulled Carson's Glock and swung it back and forth at the women. The women all shrieked in panic, ducking down and pressing themselves back against the porch wall.

"Stop or I'll shoot!" Her hand shook as she moved the gun back and forth across the group. "You." She pointed at the boy—"You! Get over there with them."

"Spencer to you."

He raised his hands over his head and inched toward the porch.

"Liz, what's going on? Have you lost your mind?" Beth implored.

"No, I've finally found it. Now shut up!"

Kandi whimpered. Anne moved toward her.

"I wouldn't do that if I were you," Liz threatened. Her voice rose hysterically.

Everything clicked in Anne's mind. Ignoring Carson's headshake, she responded, "You're smart, Liz. I have to hand it to you. You had us all fooled. When did you decide to frame Beth for her husband's death? In fact, I bet you actually wrote that note."

"Smart thinking, Sherlock." But you've got some of it wrong. Edward wasn't the intended victim. *She* was." Liz thrust out her arm and pointed the gun at Beth.

Beth cried out, "What! But, why? Why?" She clutched at her throat.

"You're so stupid. Edward and I were lovers. He promised me he was going to leave you. Why I ever believed him . . . I should have known . . . so stupid. He used me," She spat out. "I hated him. He thought he was so clever." She laughed maniacally.

"As soon as Jake goes off to college," she mimicked a male voice. "So much for promises!" Her hand shook as the gun became heavier and her palm started sweating. She released the hold on Kandi and gripped the gun with both hands. "Don't try anything or I'll shoot. Give me the keys."

"I, I, *like*, left them in the ignition."

"Then go start the truck. And no funny business or I shoot one of your friends."

Kandi went over and started the truck and Liz motioned her over to join the others on the porch.

Carson kept his hands up. "I have to give it to you. I'm impressed. I'd like to hear the whole story."

"I don't think so. This isn't some cop show on TV."

"Indulge me. I can tell you must have a plan, or you would know that you can't make it out of the city limits."

"You're right there. I am smart. I plan everything." She waved the gun at the women on the porch.

The women ducked lower, flinching and afraid.

Liz spoke, "All the time we were in college, they looked down on me. They thought they were the smart ones. But my IQ beats all of theirs. Genius level!"

The thought of the line between genius and insanity sprung to Anne's mind. She watched as Carson instructed Kandi to move behind him. Soon, Kandi had made it to the steps that led down to the yard. Anne reached over and motioned for Kandi to join her. She clutched Kandi close to her, trying to move the girl behind her and out of the line of fire.

Liz snickered. "Oh, Taylor. I played you like a fiddle. l knew you'd work your magic and get Lil to come. I also knew that would make Beth go ballistic. She'd want to leave. At that point Eddie would be off skiing and out of the way. She would take the car and sadly, she'd become ill or maybe her brakes would fail. Then she'd pull a Thelma and Louise only without Louise going along for the ride.

"But then everything changed. I overheard him telling Lil he would leave Beth for her." She shook her head and laughed hysterically. "Can you believe it? The joke was on me. All this time. I waited, thinking he really loved me. But he only ever loved *her*." She pointed the gun at Lil who fell to her knees, crying.

"I had to make him pay. He'd used all of us. All of us! No more." She wiped her hand on her pants and then gripped the gun tighter. "It was so simple. I'd made up a tincture with foxglove. I'd been giving it to Edward in tiny doses, never too much. I wasn't sure if he would notice the different taste. Plus, everyone needed to think his heart condition was worsening." She laughed again. "Which it was. Helped along by me and my helpful suggestion to switch to a vape pen. Easy to replace the liquid with my own concoction."

Beth exclaimed, "So that's why he'd been complaining of stomach issues. Even here he was sick after we went out to eat. Plus, the hand tremors. They were becoming more pronounced. He said it was going to affect his practice."

"I figured if you could see he wouldn't be able to work, that you'd leave the marriage." She shook her head at Beth. "I tried everything I could to get you to leave him."

"Why wouldn't you have just done what needed to be done!" Liz yelled and took a step toward Beth. "But no, you're so weak. And greedy. You never loved him. You loved the concept of him. That's why you put up with his horrible treatment of you and his affairs that he threw in your face. For years I've been trying to get you to see the truth. But you're so stupid."

Tears streamed down Beth's cheeks. "But I thought we were friends."

"You thought wrong."

The boy spoke up, "I saw you."

"Spencer, hush." Carson stuck his hand out across the boy's chest and forced Spencer behind him.

"What do you mean?" She squinted at the boy. "Spit it out, Spencer."

"I hid in the priest hole in the hallway."

"Priest hole?" Everyone echoed.

He nodded. "It's a pretty cool hiding place. You can see everyone coming and going. I saw you go into their room with one of those vials in your hand. Then you came out and you still had it. After you all went for your walk I went in your room. The vial was there, but it was almost empty."

Liz frowned. "You're a nosey little twerp."

"Does that mean you've been in the house all along?" Taylor asked Spencer.

"Yep. I ran away, you know, from the foster home and some kids told me about this old place. They used to come here, you know, after Mister Rogers died. I noticed people working on it, but they'd leave at night, so I snuck in and stayed up in the attic."

Kandi turned to him. "That explains, *like,* a lot. You're the one who's been stealing the food?"

Spencer shrugged his shoulders sheepishly. "I was, you know, hungry."

Liz took a step toward the truck. "Well, this has been fun, but needs must and all that."

"Wait." Anne moved to the steps. "What about Marie?"

"Ahhh, Marie. Collateral damage." Liz backed toward the truck. "I knew that woman was nosey, but I couldn't know what she'd heard from my conversation with Beth. You know the old saying about curiosity killing the cat."

"You tried to make it look like an accident," Spencer said. "I grabbed her right before she fell down the stairs."

"Ahhh, that makes sense now. You're the pesky ghost then?"

Spencer stuck his hands deep in his pockets. "Everyone kept talking about ghosts, so I thought if I went out at night and people saw the sheet, you know, they'd think I *was* a ghost. And it worked too, until he came along." He pointed at Carson.

"It was a glitch, you saving that nosey woman. But you actually did me a favor because then I could point the finger at Beth by spiking my own drink. I knocked Marie's glass over and then switched places."

Hope finally joined the conversation. "How did you know that Marie would be sitting next to you?"

"Psychology. That's how." She laughed. "That was my specialty. People are creatures of habit. Once they start sitting somewhere they tend to go back to those same places. We sat at those same seats for breakfast and lunch. I had to make sure Marie didn't take Edward's place, so I made sure that everyone would ask Anne and Hope to join us. Of course, I acted like they might want to do something different."

Anne thought back over the weekend. Liz was right. Everything had been one play on another with no one the wiser. Liz had even yelled at the dinner table that someone had tried to kill her, thus deflecting the suspicion away from her and onto the others.

Liz faced the group. "Now it's time to say goodbye."

"You're never going to get away with it." Anne grabbed the rail tighter as her foot began aching. "Why don't you just give yourself up? There's no way you'll go free, now that we all know your story."

The guttural laugh from Liz caused everyone to cringe.

"Really? You don't think I haven't thought this through. My escape Plan A to Plan Z? I've plotted this six ways to Sunday. My only regret is that Edward died before I got to do what I should have done long ago."

She pointed the gun at Lil.

Lil pleaded, "Please, no. My children."

Carson stepped in front of Lil. "You're not going to hurt anybody."

"Sheriff, I appreciate all your heroics, but I've already killed. I won't hesitate to shoot you."

"That may be the case but you're not going to hurt anybody." Carson took a step forward.

Spencer whistled. Caught off guard by the noise, Liz swiveled toward a huge brown animal bounding across the snow. As she raised the gun, Spencer lunged from the porch and pushed her down. The gun flew from Liz's hand.

As Liz struggled to get up from the deep snow, Spencer called off the slobbering Newfoundland. He pulled a piece of jerky out of his pocket. "Good boy. Good boy, Bear."

Chapter Twenty-Two

As Carson struggled with Liz, Hope ran down and retrieved the gun from where it had landed in the snow. Taylor bent down and helped a shaking Lil to her feet. Beth stood clutching at the post holding up the porch roof. Kandi moved beside Anne as they watched the chaos.

"That is, literally, *like*, something you see in a movie."

"Get off me. Let me go!" Liz screamed as Carson pulled handcuffs from his belt.

The wail of sirens were heard approaching the house. Anne watched as a deputy's cruiser pulled up behind Kandi's still running truck. He flung open the door, drew his gun, and jogged over to Carson and a struggling Liz.

After assessing that Carson had Liz restrained, he holstered his weapon.

Carson spoke, "Here, Ruiz. Read this lady her rights and take her in. I've got a few things to finish here, then I'll join you at headquarters."

Deputy Ruiz recited the Miranda warning as he shuffled Liz off to the cruiser.

Hope handed Carson his gun and climbed back up on the porch. Spencer, down in the snow and tightly hugging the eighty-pound puppy, gazed up at Carson.

Carson pointed toward the house. "You. Inside."

Spencer got up and the Newfoundland followed obediently. "Bear, down." The dog went to a corner by a chair and rested his big furry head on his paws.

As Carson made his way onto the porch, Hope reached over and touched his arm. "Sheriff, if it's okay with you, I think we could all use a breather to digest everything before you lay into Spencer."

"Fair enough," He responded. "I could go for a cup of coffee."

"I'm on it." Kandi, always her ever-bubbly self, even after cheating death, grinned broadly.

Anne hobbled inside, her foot pulsing with pain now. "Owwww," She moaned.

Taylor slung her arm around Anne's waist, and pulled Anne to her side. "You lean on me. Liz was right about one thing. I'm thinking you may have broken your foot, Anne. We need to take you in for an x-ray to check it out."

A shaken Beth and Lil clung to each other as they went back into the house. Lil sat quietly as Hope dialed Sam. She knew the ladies had experienced a traumatic shock and would need to be checked out. Beth sat at the end of the table, silent tears streaming down her face. Anne felt an ache in her heart for the woman whose marriage and friendship with Liz had been nothing but lies.

No one spoke as Carson pointed to a fretting Spencer to take a seat. He then walked toward the back room and when he returned he was in full gear, his Glock secured back in its holster.

"That was, *like,* crazy." Kandi finally broke the silence. "She could have killed us all."

A huge sob came from Lil who was now trembling with the shock. Beth reached over and laid her hand on Lil's. The shaken woman looked up and both had tears in their eyes.

"I'm so sorry, Lil. All this time I hated you because of the lies Liz had told me about you. I'm ashamed to admit that I believed everything she ever told me. She—and Edward too—must have thought I was such a fool." The tears spilled down her cheeks.

"It's not your fault," Taylor interjected. She was crying too. Anne could feel tears welling up in her eyes as she watched the trio mending long broken fences.

"Taylor's right, Beth. She manipulated all of us." Lil reached over and hugged Beth.

"I'm so sorry about Edward. I had no idea Liz was like that."

Beth rubbed her arms. "I really don't know how to feel right now. Certainly, I'm sad. But . . . and this will sound horrible . . . or maybe not, now that you know what I've had to deal with, but I'm a bit relieved. He'd become such a bully. Every day when he was around was a trial. I lived on pins and needles. Now I wonder if Liz wasn't giving him something that made him that way."

Kandi helped Hope put hot cups of coffee in front of everyone.

"I don't know what happened to her or when. She always seemed nice, but maybe she's been a manipulator the entire time we've known her. I never would have forgiven myself if she'd have hurt any of ya'll." Taylor choked back a sob.

Beth wiped her face. "And you, young man," She pointed to Spencer. "You nearly scared me half to death."

Spencer looked at the group from underneath his messy russet bangs.

With everyone's attention on Spencer, Carson took charge, "Spill it."

"She was going to shoot so I—"

Carson flipped a chair and sat down. "No. From the beginning. You know social services and Mrs. Laurence are going crazy looking for you."

"All she cares about is the monthly check she gets," He muttered.

"Don't be disrespectful to your elders," Carson said.

"Um, yes sir." He swept his bangs out of his eyes with his hand.

Kandi took a tray of various pastries out of the hot oven. "Wait, a minute, I forgot!" She pointed her finger at Spencer. "I almost, *like,* ran over you! I had to swerve and everything."

Spencer sighed and looked at Kandi sheepishly. "Okay, so at the foster home, Mrs. Laurence is okay. But she said I couldn't keep Bear. He, you know, needs me. I'm the only person he has. They were going to put him in a shelter. You know how bad those shelters are. No way I was letting that happen just because that dweeb at the house has some allergy. Plus, she said she couldn't afford to buy food for a monster." He looked at the women for sympathy. "Can you believe it? She called him a monster!"

"*Like* she literally called him a monster?" Kandi's

many bracelets jangled. She set the warm pastries down on the table where everyone helped themselves.

"Yeah, you know, she literally did." Spencer was on a roll now with all the attention. "Anyway, some other kid had also had a bad experience with a dog. I had to hear how he eats a lot, and sheds a lot, blah, blah, blah." He opened his hands up. "I had no choice. I stole some dog food. But I've paid it all back. Now Miss Patty wants me, you know, to keep helping out 'cause I'm good with tech."

Spencer continued, "I had, you know, to do *like* community service but the owner gave me some dog food. Mrs. Laurence didn't like the idea of Bear being outside, but she wouldn't let him inside. I overheard her talking to someone at a rescue place." He held up his hands with a pleading look on his face. "I had no choice. I booked it out of there. I'd heard this place was empty from some guys at school so I, you know, came here."

He looked up at Carson who nodded at the boy. "Go on."

"I figured I could hang out here for a while, you know, until I could decide what to do. It was easy to put Bear into the basement at night and then I'd go up to the attic where I had my place. That way I could look out the windows and see if that guy was coming over."

"Stewart?"

"I don't know his name. But he comes over and hangs out until she comes over." He cocked his head toward Kandi. Her face turned a bright pink as everyone turned toward her. "I think he's got a, you know, crush on her or something."

Anne asked Kandi, "I just realized, where is Stewart?"

"He took Autumn back over to Hope's place."

181

Hope said, "But if you were in the attic, how did you get down to the basement without any of us seeing you?"

"Oh, I went through the stairs."

Anne looked up from her cup. "What do you mean you went *through* the stairs?"

He looked over at Carson. "Should I show her?"

"That's fine." He took a swig from the coffee mug he held in his hand. "But then, right back here."

Kandi and Hope moved over to the stairs while Lil and Beth stayed seated.

"I want to see!" Anne exclaimed.

"Come on, then, I gotcha." Taylor helped Anne to her feet. Anne hopped to the back stairs.

Spencer motioned for Anne and the other ladies to wait at the bottom of the stairs while he and Hope went upstairs. At the top, he pulled on the iron knob at the end of the railing. In front of the group, a set of three stairs opened up.

"Way cool!" Kandi squeezed by Anne and went up a couple of steps to look inside the opening. Hope and Spencer had come down the stairs and joined the others. Spencer pulled a headlamp from his pocket.

"So that's where that went to." Hope rolled her eyes.

He shrugged his shoulders and turned it on, pointing it down to where a ladder was attached to a wall.

"You take that ladder and you end up in the basement."

With Taylor's help, Anne knelt on the bottom steps and peeked into the dark crevice. "Hope, did you know the house had this?"

"No. This is the first I'd seen it." She turned to Spencer. "How did you find out about it?"

"I'd been in the upstairs bathroom when I thought I'd heard someone coming up the stairs. I had to get out quick, so I ran over to the backstairs. I almost fell when I grabbed the handle and pulled on it. Then, you know, the stairs popped open."

"That is, *like,* so cool." Kandi clasped her hands.

Hope stepped back so Spencer could shut up the opening in the stairs. He let it drop.

"There's our slamming noise!" Anne and Hope spoke in unison.

"A few times I had to hurry, so I didn't get to close it easy."

Carson appeared at the bottom of the steps behind the women. "Okay, we need to get back to the business at hand."

Hope was now assisting Anne back over to the table. "What business?"

"Do you all want to press charges against young Spencer here for trespassing?"

"Let me have a word with my partners," Hope responded. While Carson sat there with his arms crossed, she continued, "If you and Spencer could wait in the living room for a few minutes, that would be helpful."

"Fine." Carson nodded and put his hand on Spencer's shoulder. The boy slouched off dejectedly toward the other room, like a man headed for the gallows.

A course of action was quickly agreed upon, and Spencer was brought back into the kitchen. Hope addressed Spencer, "We're not going to press charges. You did try to save Marie's life and you acted, though not the best idea at the time, to stop Liz. That shows a lot of bravery."

Spencer grinned.

"However," Hope continued.

The smile left his face.

"We do believe Spencer needs to do some community service since he's been eating our food—"

"Your cooking is, you know, really good." Spencer addressed Kandi.

"*Like*, thanks." She beamed.

Anne took over for Hope and continued to address Spencer. "We expect you to come after school and then also on the weekends to help out. We'll have you do chores like clearing snow, dog walking—"

"Dog walking?" He perked up at that.

Kandi came over and handed Spencer another pastry. "We've been thinking that we could use a dog around here at night to keep critters away—the four-legged *and* the two-legged kind. If you think it's okay, we'd like Bear to stay here."

"That's awesome!" Spencer, forgetting his role as a tough teenager, ran over and hugged her.

He turned to Hope and Anne. "I'll work really hard. You wait and see."

"Good to hear it," Hope responded. "But no more stealing. Deal?"

"Deal." He went over and held out his hand, which she shook.

A knock on the door announced the arrival of Mrs. Laurence and Sam. Carson escorted Spencer out, and Anne heard him telling the foster mom about Spencer's community service and the agreement for Bear to stay at the Inn.

Sam listened to the story and asked Beth to join him in the dining room. After Beth and Sam had left the room, Taylor sat down next to Anne.

Taylor leaned toward Anne, "Is it just me or does that guy smell like popcorn?"

"Yes," Anne said. "It's a bit of a story."

"Go 'head. Gimme the real enchilada. Which if you think about it, makes no sense as a saying because who's going to say, 'give me the fake enchilada'!" Taylor laughed. "Wait, a minute, that sounds really good. Who wants enchiladas?"

Laughter took over and for a few moments, the women struggled to keep straight faces. Tears mingled with laughter, and Anne knew it was the release of all the stress.

"How about this? We'll grab some enchiladas in town before you all head out to Denver."

Hope joined Sam in the other room and checked over Lil and Beth to ensure they were okay for travel after the shock.

Taylor grinned as she returned from the living room. "I just got to add that we should invite Mister Popcorn to come with us. He almost makes you want to be sick, so he can care for you."

Sam returned to the kitchen, EMS bag in his hand. He spent some time visiting with the ladies before heading out for another call.

Everyone agreed that enchiladas sounded like a good suggestion. Hope called and made a reservation at Abuela's Cocina for a late lunch. After Carson and another deputy took formal statements from everyone, the women went upstairs to pack.

Lunch was subdued, but everyone ate heartily.

Taylor and Lil agreed that they'd like to come back under better circumstances, while not surprisingly, Beth declined a free return stay.

Chapter Twenty-Three

After they had seen the women off, Anne sat in the Inn's living room, her bandaged foot and leg propped on a footstool. Hope had called Autumn over to the house to help put things back in order. Anne listened to the muffled music playing overhead.

The back door opened, and Anne heard heavy boots moving across the kitchen floor.

"In here," Anne called out.

Carson walked into the hallway. He was no longer wearing his uniform but still looked imposing and strong. He took off his Stetson and held it in his hand.

She waved him over to a seat close to her.

"Come in. It looks like this foot is going to be pretty worthless for a bit."

"Broken?"

"Hopefully not. I'm going over to the urgent care to get an x-ray to confirm it, but Hope's pretty sure I only twisted my ankle badly."

"Well, that's good news." He sat hunched on the seat, his arms perched on his knees.

"I have to ask you one thing." Anne shifted in her seat to put less pressure on her ankle.

"Yes?"

"How were you so confident Liz wasn't going to shoot any of us?"

"Well, ND . . . "

"ND?"

"You know, Nancy Drew. You didn't want me calling you Nancy, so I figured I'd call you ND. It's where it pays to go by facts instead of supposition."

"What do you mean?"

"The first thing I noticed was her deceptive behavior when we were talking with everyone. Did you notice that she was the only one to point the finger at Beth?"

"Well, yes, but we didn't know if her story was any truer than any of the others."

"Ahhh, but here's where some training comes in handy."

Anne crossed her arms. "Okay, enlighten me. What training?"

"Interrogation practices regarding lies and deception."

"Such as?"

"Steepling for one."

"Steepling . . . what do you mean?"

"Liz steepled her fingers when she talked to us." Carson held his hands in front of him with his fingers, creating a little steeple. "That's a subconscious sign that she feels smarter than the person she's talking to. In this case, me."

"Interesting. Okay, I get that, but Liz also said she denied having anything to do with Edward's or Marie's murder."

"Yes, but denial isn't the same as not admitting guilt."

Anne leaned forward. "Say again?"

"I can deny something but that doesn't mean I didn't do it. It's just that I refuse to admit to it. It's deflection."

"Ohhhh, that *is* interesting." Anne grimaced as she lifted her leg and tilted her foot.

"Need another pillow?"

"Yes, please."

Carson rose from his seat, crossed over to the sofa and pulled a pillow from the couch. He returned and motioned for Anne to lift her leg. As she grabbed her calf with both hands, he gingerly set the pillow on top of the other one already in place.

"Better?"

She laid her foot down. "Yes, much. Thanks."

"Okay, there were some signs that I didn't catch. But I did catch one really, really, big sign. She had your gun and could have killed us all," said Anne.

"No, Liz wouldn't have harmed or killed anyone that way."

"Why do you say that?"

"First, it was evident that Liz has never held a gun before."

"How did you know that?"

"Because after I put the gun in the office, I removed the magazine and emptied the chamber. If she knew guns, she would have immediately known the gun had no bullets."

"Oh, okay. Of course. That makes sense. But she

could have still done something."

"Don't worry. I had it under control." He patted a bulge near his ankle.

Oh of course, he carried more than one gun. Anne nodded to show she understood. "Okay, but that still begs the question, how did she get the gun out of my locked office and cabinet?"

He smiled. "Hypothetically?"

"Yes, hypothetically." She returned the smile.

"Think about it. I'd told both you and Hope to lock the back staircase door. But then later, we would find that the door would be unlocked. I knew that someone was either using your keys, had another set, or was picking the locks. Turned out that Liz was pretty proficient at lock picking."

"What will happen to her now?"

"They've called in a psychiatrist who will do testing and provide a diagnosis. After that, it's up to the court to decide." He rose and wiped off his pant legs.

"Just thought I'd stop by and check in to make sure everyone here is okay."

"Yes, I'm sure it will be a while before the reality of all this settles in." She scooted to a better position.

"Okay then, goodbye." He picked up his hat and made for the door.

"Wait!" She struggled to sit up straighter. "I think if you're going to call me names like ND, and after all we've been through, what should I call you?"

"Carson. But you can call me Sheriff." He tipped his hat, smiled and walked out the door.

Anne fumed. What a piece of work. That man.

His footsteps halted.

Anne looked up at the opening to the hall.

Carson stood there, hat in hand. "Hypothetically,

what would you say about me calling you next week?"
Anne grinned. Hypothetical just got real.

Epilogue

Marie's celebration of life service was held the following Wednesday. Kandi helped Anne, who wore a boot to brace her ankle, while using a cane that old man Stanley had loaned her. When the service was over, Anne, Hope, and Kandi watched as the vehicles began their procession to the cemetery on the edge of town.

Anne looked up to see Pat standing outside her shop and Spencer standing next to her. He waved and pointed at his new haircut. Since his escapades at the Brandywine Inn, and his part in helping catch a killer, he had become a bit of a town hero. There was a front-page piece on him in the local paper, "Local Boy Saves the Day", and an article in the *Denver Post* about foster care and the need for more foster parents. He was now a minor celebrity in town and was milking his fifteen minutes.

Anne glanced at her watch. "I guess we should get over to the hall and set out the food for when everyone arrives back from the graveside."

"I've got everything ready." She motioned to Spencer, who was wearing a white shirt and black slacks.

"You're looking mighty spiffy there, Spencer. Thanks for helping out." Hope squeezed his shoulder.

"I really do feel sorry I couldn't have saved Marie."

"It wasn't your fault. It wasn't anyone's fault," Anne replied.

Kandi chimed in, "You want to, *like,* ride with me over to the hall?"

"Sure, you know, I really like what you did," said Spencer.

The pair continued their conversation as they made their way to the truck.

"I think we did the right thing by him." Hope helped Anne to her car.

Anne lowered herself into the passenger seat. "I agree. I think he's essentially a good kid and just needed someone to take some interest in him."

After Anne had pulled her leg into the car, Hope shut the door behind her. She moved around the front of the car and slid behind the driver's wheel. "Not only is he a good kid. He's smart too. Have you seen what he's done with the reservation page on the Inn's website? Calendar? The pictures?" She started the car. "It's made a huge difference in how much easier it is to navigate."

"That's great. I'll take a look." She shifted toward Hope who put the car in reverse. "On another subject, I got a call from Taylor. She's been to see Liz."

"Really?"

"Yes, she told me that after Liz had her psychotic break, the DA is recommending incarceration at a secured mental facility." Anne sighed. "Sad, really. Her victims, her friends . . . everyone will have to live with what she did."

"On a happier subject, what's Taylor up to?"

"She is quitting her job."

"Is that so?" Hope turned on her blinker.

"Yes, she says she's tired with being around death all the time, she's ready to be around life for a while."

"I can certainly understand that." Anne smoothed down the fabric of her dress. "What's she going to do?"

"She's not sure yet but she's saved up a lot of money, so she's planning on spending some time out in Comfort."

"I don't blame her. I like being in comfort too."

Hope laughed. "Oh sorry. No, not comfort. It's a town in Texas. Comfort. Her dad owns a little ranch with a lot of acreage where she keeps her horses. She's going to take a month or two off and try to figure out what she wants to do with the rest of her life."

"Well, good for her." Anne saw lots of cars with people getting out and headed into the hall. "She say anything about Beth or Lil?"

"Lil has gone back to her work at the university and research lab. Beth is selling the big house and is volunteering at a women's shelter. Her son has returned to college."

"I'm sure they've been affected by everything and it will be a while before they can really come to terms with what happened."

"Yes, that's true." Hope parked the car by a side door.

As Anne emerged from her side, she spied Sheriff Carson. He waved to her and motioned for her to wait for a minute.

"I'll see you inside." Hope walked to the side door and, glancing back, gave Anne a quick thumbs-up.

"Ms. Freemont."

"Are we back to full names, Sheriff?" She squinted up at him.

"I wanted to let you know why I haven't called. I've been busy working a case—"

A woman's lyrical voice cut through the air. "Carson."

Anne looked as Sorcha approached and then back up to the Sheriff.

"I see. No worries. To be honest, I'd totally forgotten all about it."

"But . . . "

"I'm sure you're busy. I'm busy too. In fact, I just don't know when I'll have any free time." She shrugged. "I've got to go inside and help with the sandwiches."

"All the best with your . . . case." She stole a glance toward Sorcha, the woman's fiery red hair cascading down her shoulders.

Anne wished she could quickly turn her back on the man, but all she could do was limp away and hope she looked halfway decorous.

Inside, she closed the door behind her and stayed in the cool, dark hallway for a minute to collect her thoughts.

I'm not ready for that stuff anyway. What happened was simply due to the situation. Better this way. No way I can compete with Miss Celtic Sophia Loren.

She smoothed down her dress again and walked over to where Hope and Kandi were plating sandwiches. Spencer and Autumn were down by the drinks, handing out cups filled with ice.

"Hello? Hello!" A short, stout woman headed their way.

"I'm Marie's sister. I want to say thank you for

everything you've done for us. I know Marie thought the world of you both."

Gulp. Anne wondered if Hope also felt a rock in the pit of her stomach.

"Anyway, I have something for you." She turned around and motioned to a man that mirrored her in size and demeanor. In his hand, he held a box.

He set the box down on the table and opened it up. Inside, cradled with towels was a decanter of Marie's award-winning elderberry cordial.

The woman pursed her lips and her husband handed her a white handkerchief. She dotted her eyes with it. "There's only a few of these left, and I know Marie would have wanted you all to have one."

"You really shouldn't have," Anne replied.

"No, I know that's what she would have wanted. Thank you again." She sniffled, and her husband led her away.

It wasn't long before the crowd thinned, and they were left to clear up the hall.

Hope and Anne stared down at the box. Kandi, Spencer, and Autumn joined the pair.

"What is it?" Autumn asked.

"It's Marie's cordial."

Spencer picked it up from the box. "Oh, I've heard it's really, you know, good. You want some?"

"Pass!" Anne and Hope squealed.

From the Author

I hope you enjoyed reading *Cordial Killing*. Would you mind doing me a big favor and reviewing it on your favorite places on social media or review sites as well as sharing it with your friends?

Are you interested in backyard farming or what I like to call it—suburban homesteading?

https://www.facebook.com/havensteader

You want to know about my other books or connect through Facebook?

https://facebook.com/VikkiWaltonAuthor

Finally, you can contact me directly:

vikki@vikkiwalton.com

Writing is a solitary process, but it often involves lots of input from many people. I want to acknowledge a few of them here:

First, a big thanks to future author, Spencer Stepp, who helped guide me in what a young boy might be like and what he would be reading. Unlike the Spencer in my story, he has two loving parents, Steve and Nancy.

Next to my friend, Kris Burgoyne, who introduced me to Roxann Stark Ross. Roxann gave me a tour of her Victorian home and her home's surprising feature, which I had to include in this story.

A thank you to Valerie Blankenship of Sage Women Herbs who helped me talk through the feasibility of deadly tinctures. At least, after I assured her it was for my book.

Of course, a book's cover and interior are extremely important. Erika Parker Rogers did the wonderful book cover illustration and Melinda Martin pulled it all together once again to make a beautiful cover. The formatting was completed by Rik Hall.

After your eyes blur together from reading the same thing over and over, you realize how important an editor is for catching those gaffs and goofs. Jennifer Bradshaw of Balancing Act Editing made the process so much easier. Any errors are mine—all mine.

Many others helped me along the way and while their names are not written here, they are greatly appreciated.

Finally, dear reader, thank you. I don't think that readers realize what a blessing they are to authors. You encourage every author to keep writing. Thank you.

Made in the USA
Monee, IL
08 December 2020

51394482R00121